"I need to be on my way...

"No need to get up. I'll see myself out."

"No, no. I'll see you out," Kristin protested.

But her feet tangled up in the hem of her dress and she pitched forward. Jackson moved swiftly, catching her in his arms before she pitched face-first onto the carpet.

Her breasts crushed against him and his arms wrapped tight around her body. Through the satin of her gown, she felt the imprint of his fingers, the heat of his palms against her back. And, darn her, she liked it.

Kristin looked up into Jackson's fiercely glittering blue eyes, shocked by what she saw there. Passion. Heat.

A groan ripped from Jackson's throat before he lowered his face to hers and captured her lips. Shock coursed through her body at the long-missed and all too familiar touch of his mouth on hers.

Shock and desire and a need to kiss him back...with all the pent-up frustration and sorrow she'd borne alone for far too long.

* * *

What Happens at Christmas... by Yvonne Lindsay is part of the Clashing Birthrights series.

Dear Reader,

Welcome to book three in my Clashing Birthrights series—
What Happens at Christmas.... I love a reunion story,
especially when I'm writing it. So many angles to cover and
utilize as my couple find their way back to love.

Trust doesn't come easily to Kristin Richmond, especially
after discovering her adored father had deceived his whole
family by leading a double life. She can be intense, but
she's also deeply loyal and when her trust is broken, she
doesn't hesitate to move on. Discovering she was duped
by her lover, who turned out to be a spy in her finance
department, has rocked her confidence in everyone.

When the family lawyer announces his imminent retirement
and the appointment of a new lawyer in his place, she's
skeptical about their suitability—especially when the new
lawyer turns out to be none other than her first love from
her college days. A man who promised her forever, then
left her without a word.

Jackson Jones keeps his past deeply under wraps, but
he quickly recognizes that he's going to have to open old
wounds if he is to earn Kristin's trust and remain in his role
as her family's lawyer. Getting this right is important to him,
but realizing that his attraction to Kristin never went away
makes working closely with her a new level of torture.
Can he earn her trust without ruining the fragile friendship
they manage to rebuild, or will their mutual attraction and
his secrets eventually drive a permanent wedge between
them?

Will Jackson be able to prove that he is the kind of man
Kristin can rely on, or will he let her down again? Read on
to find out!

Best wishes,

Yvonne Lindsay

YvonneLindsay.com

YVONNE LINDSAY

—

WHAT HAPPENS AT CHRISTMAS...

HARLEQUIN
DESIRE

DESIRE™

ISBN-13: 978-1-335-73521-8

What Happens at Christmas...

Harlequin Enterprises ULC
22 Adelaide St. West, 40th Floor
Toronto, Ontario M5H 4E3, Canada
www.Harlequin.com

Printed in U.S.A.

Award-winning *USA TODAY* bestselling author **Yvonne Lindsay** has always preferred the stories in her head to the real world. Married to her blind-date sweetheart and with two adult children, she spends her days crafting the stories of her heart. In her spare time she can be found with her nose firmly in someone else's book.

Books by Yvonne Lindsay

Harlequin Desire

Marriage at First Sight

Tangled Vows
Inconveniently Wed
Vengeful Vows

Clashing Birthrights

Seducing the Lost Heir
Scandalizing the CEO
What Happens at Christmas...

Visit her Author Profile page at Harlequin.com, or yvonnelindsay.com, for more titles.

You can find Yvonne Lindsay on Facebook, along with other Harlequin Desire authors, at Facebook.com/harlequindesireauthors!

I dedicate this to my editor Charles and the behind-the-scenes team that helps bring my books to my readers.

One

"Mom, I'm sorry. I won't be able to make it tonight. I have too much work on my plate."

Kristin eyed the Christmas decorations that festooned her office, with a baleful eye. She wasn't lying, exactly. She did have a ton of work to get through, but she wasn't in the mood for yet another happy family gathering where everyone except her was paired up with a significant other. Normally, it didn't bother her, but lately she'd been more unsettled than usual.

"Kristin, I won't take no for an answer. I'm done with your excuses. Tonight is important to me and I expect you to be here at seven sharp."

Kristin's mom, Nancy, abruptly ended the call, leaving her daughter staring at the phone on her office desk with a mixture of frustration and curiosity. Kristin rolled her chair from her desk, pushed her hands through her long hair and massaged her scalp with her fingertips. It didn't ease the perpetual headache she'd had for the past several months.

Her identical twin brothers, Keaton and Logan, had been putting pressure on her to cut her workload, citing their father's massive fatal stroke almost a year ago as a fine example of why you shouldn't burn the candle at both ends. She was doing the work of two people at the moment since she hadn't yet been able to bring herself to replace the man she'd trusted as her right hand here at work, and as her lover in the bedroom.

And all along Isaac had been a spy working for their biggest rival, Warren Everard. While everyone involved in the corporate espionage was now facing charges, it still galled her, even all these months later, that she'd never suspected—not even for a moment—that he was capable of such subterfuge. And it made her doubly wary of replacing him   in the office, or at home. Business was hard enough right now, without worrying about having to second-guess everyone around you. It had been the easier option to simply assimilate Isaac's workload into her own. After all, it wasn't as if she had any reason to rush home.

Isaac's betrayal was doubly cruel because she hadn't shared with her family how intimate she and Isaac had become. They'd kept their relationship under wraps. Not a single person in the office had ever suspected that they were more than boss and employee. She'd technically been in a position of power over him. Forming a relationship would have been frowned upon, so when he'd suggested they initially keep things quiet, she'd been in full agreement. But all along his plan had been to abuse her trust, which was, in her book, far more damaging. And she'd borne the pain of that betrayal and her broken heart alone.

Kristin rose from her seat and turned to face the darkening sky outside her office window. The Richmond Tower commanded exceptional views of the Seattle cityscape, but she rarely took the time to appreciate it. Christmas was only a little over three weeks away but her gaze remained oblivious to the glittering outlook spread before her like a pirate's jewel casket.

Instead, her thoughts turned inward. So much had changed in the past year. Courtesy of the double life her father had successfully lived, right up until the moment he'd dropped dead in his office, she'd gained not just one brother—Logan had been kidnapped as a child and was now reunited with the family—but two half brothers, and a half sister to boot.

And while it had been a joy to watch her full brothers both find love with amazing women whom she respected and adored, seeing her brothers' happiness only made Isaac's duplicity all the more painful.

Was it too much to expect to be able to build a relationship founded on mutual attraction, affection and trust? Kristin shook her head. Apparently, for her, it was. And now she had to present a cheerful face at another family dinner. Ah, well, she thought as she returned to her computer and backed up her work, at least she could depend on a better meal than the microwave instant dinner option in her apartment's freezer. She chuckled ruefully. She sounded like a total loser.

Kristin checked that the backup was complete, grabbed her bag and coat and locked her office door behind her. She fingered her car keys, wondering if she should drive to her mom's place in Bellevue. No, she decided. She'd order a driver and leave her car in its secure parking space below the building. The way she was feeling right now, she might indulge in a glass or two of wine tonight.

Half an hour later, Kristin let herself into the large two-story mansion that had been her parents' home for as long as she could remember and shrugged off her coat. She loved coming here. There was a sense of stability about the place that she desperately craved now. The clipped sound of heels on the parquet floor alerted her to the arrival of the family housekeeper, Martha.

"Ah, Kristin. It's good to see you. Your mom and the others are in the main salon having drinks before dinner. Here, let me take your coat."

"The main salon? I thought this was a casual thing," Kristin commented as she passed her coat to the older woman.

Martha had been in her parents' employ since Kristin had been a baby and, since Kristin's father's death last year, had become more of a companion to her mom.

"Mrs. Richmond asked that I send you through when you arrived," the housekeeper continued smoothly without actually answering Kristin's question.

A sense of unease filled her. Her mom only used the main sitting room for formal occasions. What was going on? Realizing it would be useless to press Martha, who was already walking away to hang up her coat, Kristin made her way across the foyer to the double wooden doors that led to the rest of her family. A murmur of voices came through the door and she hesitated—reluctant, for some reason, to join them. A burst of laughter from inside the room motivated her to reach for the handle and join her family.

She scanned the room as she entered, noting the beautifully decorated Christmas tree her mom had erected immediately after Thanksgiving, and relaxed as she identified her brothers and their partners, her mom and Hector Ramirez. Hector was the family's attorney and had been an absolute rock of support for her mom since Douglas Richmond's sudden death. So much so, the two of them had vacationed together in Palm Springs a few months ago.

As Kristin entered the room, her mom rose from Hector's side and crossed toward her daughter to welcome her.

"I made it," Kristin said with a smile as her mom enveloped her in a loving embrace.

"Thank you, my darling girl. It's always so good to see you."

"You know, if you came back to the office we'd see each other every day."

Nancy had worked side by side with her husband until his death nearly a year ago and had been heavily involved in the family's charitable foundation. But now she rarely entered the building where he'd died and had established a base here at home to manage the Richmond Foundation remotely.

"What can I get you to drink?" Nancy asked, ignoring Kristin's not-so-subtle comment.

"My usual white wine would be great, thanks."

Kristin turned to say hi to her brothers and their partners. Logan and Honor had married in the summer and, last week at Thanksgiving, announced they were expecting a baby. While Honor wasn't showing yet, there was a glow about her that inspired a prick of envy in Kristin's heart. And the way Logan looked at Honor these days? Well, his love for her and their child was tangible. More than anything Kristin ached to have that level of commitment with someone else.

Keaton and Tami were equally tightly knit. They'd originally started as an office romance at Richmond Developments, but Tami now worked as a project manager and liaison between the Richmond Foundation and other charities on special ventures. Tami rose from her seat and hugged Kristin in greeting.

"I was hoping you would make it," Tami said with a welcoming smile. "We hardly get to see you outside of work these days."

"Do you know what this is all about?" Kristin whispered to her.

"Not a clue. It doesn't quite feel like Nancy's regular family dinner vibe, does it?"

"True," Kristin conceded. She couldn't quite shake the apprehension that niggled at the back of her mind.

Her mom returned with Kristin's glass of wine and then turned and faced the room. Some silent communication must have passed between her and Hector, because he rose and stood next to her, one arm casually draped around Nancy's waist.

"If I could have all your attention, please," Nancy started, sounding a little nervous.

That niggle in the back of Kristin's mind grew stronger.

"Hector and I have an announcement to make. As you know, we've been friends for many years and he's been an incredible support to me since Douglas passed away. In fact, he's become so important to me that I can't see my future without him…and I'm very proud to tell you that he has consented to be my husband."

There was a sudden murmur in the room and Kristin felt her stomach twist in a knot.

"You asked Hector to marry you?" she blurted.

"He was too much of a gentleman to do it so soon after your father's death. But if Douglas's passing taught me anything, it was to grab hold of what's important and keep it close to you. I didn't want to waste any more time following other people's expectations or beating around the bush." Nancy turned and faced Hector and beamed at him, her love for him radiating from her. "I love him and that's why I asked him to marry me. He said yes and I couldn't be happier."

The others rose from their seats, offering their congratulations and hugging Nancy and shaking Hector's hand, but Kristin stood on the periphery. Nancy extricated herself from the rest of the family and came over to Kristin.

"Kristin? Aren't you happy for us?" she asked, a worried frown pulling at her brows.

"Isn't it a bit soon, Mom? Dad hasn't even been dead a year. I mean, I have nothing against Hector and I know how much he's come to mean to you, but don't you think you're rushing things?"

Nancy laughed and patted Kristin's arm. "Oh, my darling. We're both nearing sixty. We want to spend the rest of our lives together, properly, as husband and wife. It's important to us both and I trust Hector. He would never let me down the way your father did. Seriously, Kristin, you wouldn't stand in the way of our happiness, would you?"

Kristin hesitated. Of course she wanted her mom to be happy.

Hector joined them. "Everything okay, ladies?" he asked.

"Everything is fine," Nancy assured him and gave Kristin a look that brooked no argument. "Isn't it, Kristin?"

"Yes, absolutely," Kristin said, forcing a smile to her face. She still couldn't put a finger on why she felt uncomfortable. Sour grapes because everyone around her was paired up and living their happily-ever-afters and she wasn't? She raised her glass. "Congratulations to you both. May you be exceptionally happy together."

"Thank you, Kristin," Hector said, his eyes glistening with moisture. "It means a great deal to us to hear you say that. We understand how close you were to your father and how much you miss him. He was my best friend but I can't deny that I've loved Nancy for many years and I feel privileged to be able to plan the rest of our lives as one."

His words struck Kristin to her core. There was no doubt Hector's feelings for Nancy were genuine.

"And what about your work for us, Hector? Will you remain our family attorney?" she asked.

"I'm glad you asked." He smiled. "It leads us to our second announcement for this evening. I've decided to take early retirement—I sold my practice to a longtime friend and colleague. To facilitate a smooth takeover, I will remain on in an advisory capacity for the next six months."

"A longtime friend? Who?" Kristin pressed. "Have we met him before?"

"I don't believe so," Hector replied.

"Then how can we be sure he'll be a good fit for us? How can we trust him?"

She spoke the words without thinking. Hector was saved from answering by the echoing tones of the front doorbell.

"Well, it sounds as if he's arrived to join us, so you

can find out the answers to those questions yourself," Hector said with a confident smile.

Kristin helped herself to a generous swig of her wine. While the fine vintage was like a kiss of velvet on her tongue, it burned all the way to her stomach, reminding her she hadn't eaten much today. She didn't like the sound of any of this. What if the new person wasn't good enough? Their family had been through hell and back these past several months, first with Logan popping out of the woodwork thirty-four years after his abduction as a baby, then her dad dying, then the discovery that he had a another family and business mirroring theirs on the other side of the country. After that there'd been the corporate espionage, of which Isaac had been an integral part.

How could they be expected to trust a stranger?

"Darling, don't worry so much. Hector's friend has an exceptional reputation," her mom murmured in her ear.

"He'd better have," Kristin muttered before taking another sip of her wine.

She turned to face the sitting room doors as they swung open. Martha announced the new arrival.

"Mr. Jones has arrived," she said before ushering him through.

Logan and Keaton had moved forward and obstructed her immediate line of sight to the newcomer.

"Good evening, everyone. I hope I'm not late?"

The man's voice was deep and resonant and there was something disturbingly familiar about it. The niggle in Kristin's mind morphed into a full-blown sense of misgiving.

"No, not at all," Hector hastened to assure him. "Everyone, please welcome my good friend Jackson Jones."

And there he stood. All six feet three inches of him clad in bespoke Armani and, according to her accelerated heart rate, looking even more fiercely attractive than she remembered. His dark blue eyes focused on her with laser precision. His nostrils flared ever so slightly on a sharply indrawn breath.

Jackson Jones.

The first man she'd ever loved.

The first man she'd ever slept with.

The man who'd walked out on her without a single word or a backward glance.

The man she'd sworn to hate for eternity.

Two

Shock plummeted through him like an intensive bolt of electricity. Jackson forced himself to scan the room and smile as if catching a glimpse of Kristin Richmond hadn't just been an apocalyptic blast from the past. He eyed the faces of the assembled family group. Hector stepped forward and pumped his hand in greeting, and pulled a beautiful older woman forward to meet him.

"Jackson, glad you could make it. This is my fiancée, Nancy Richmond. Nancy, this is Jackson Jones. You've heard me talk about him at length and I'm glad you now get to finally meet him."

Jack bent his head and took the woman's hand. "It's a pleasure to meet you," he intoned smoothly.

All along, he was aware of the burning imprint

of Kristin's gaze on the back of his head. As if he was the target and her eyes a nocked arrow in a bow. Kristin had never spoken in detail about her family but she had said she only had one brother and Hector had told him this family had no less than six adult children. Richmond wasn't such an unusual name, but of all the Richmond families in the world he had to fall into this one? Seemed like karma really was a bitch.

He focused his attention on his host and hostess with some difficulty, yet remained constantly aware of the younger woman on the periphery of the room.

"And you, too, Mr. Jones," Nancy replied.

"Please, call me Jackson, or Jack."

"Jackson, then. Come, meet my family."

Nancy effected introductions to the two identical males standing just behind her. Jack studied them carefully, knowing he'd probably be tested at some stage on being able to tell them apart. He was relieved to note that Logan had a small chicken pox scar above his right eyebrow, and made a mental note to remember that tiny detail. The men's partners came next and then the final family member in the room came forward. As his gaze alighted on her features, the air in Jack's lungs deserted him.

Kristin Richmond. Every cell in his body lurched to unwelcome attention. The physical memory of how it had felt to touch her reared up from the darkest recesses of his mind. She'd always had the softest skin—everywhere. And her scent had been something he'd never fully forgotten, no matter how much guilt or time had passed. He dragged in a breath and let it go slowly. They hadn't seen each other since the day they'd graduated college. The day that had started as his proudest but had rapidly become his most shameful day, ever. He extended his hand to her.

"Ms. Richmond, it's good to see you," he said.

"Is it?" she answered sharply.

The strain around her eyes showed she was as shocked to see him in her family home as he was to discover her family was his newest client. Between finalizing the decision to accept Hector's offer, buying a house here and moving from California as well as moving into the offices and meeting the staff, Jackson hadn't yet had time to read the files for all his new clients. Hector had failed to mention the names of all the members in the Richmond family and, to his cost, Jackson hadn't had time to research them fully before meeting them, either. That was something he would definitely amend the second he returned to his office.

"Kristin!" her mom admonished in horrified tones. "We don't speak to our guests like that. I'm sorry, Mr. Jones—Jackson—I assure you I brought her up to have better manners than that."

Nancy laughed awkwardly but Kristin wasn't giving an inch. She also wasn't giving him her hand, so he let his drop uselessly to his side and fought the urge to clench it in frustration.

"Mr. Jones and I knew each other in college,"

Kristin said to her mother before returning her attention to him.

Her clear, gray eyes bored into him like lasers.

"I didn't know you'd changed to law. But then again, you never did tell me what you were doing."

To anyone else her words could almost have sounded as if she were teasing, but there was a barb there that would pierce armor plating. She hadn't forgiven him for disappearing from her life the way he had. He didn't blame her for it, either. What he'd done was unconscionable, but he'd had damn good reasons. Reasons he simply couldn't articulate at that time. Reasons he wasn't in a hurry to go into under the current circumstances, either. He looked into her eyes and for the briefest second lost himself in the memory of her. She'd always been a passionate woman, even when angry. That hadn't changed.

Hector interrupted them before he could say anything, offering him a drink. Jack accepted a glass of mineral water—he needed to keep his wits about him with Kristin shooting daggers at him. He knew that he was going to have to make a long overdue apology to her. He should have done it years ago, but after his parents scandalous deaths it had been easier to walk away and leave the wreckage of his old life behind, even if that meant leaving Kristin behind, too.

What he'd done then was wrong, and it was clear, from the way she obviously still harbored a grudge, that he'd hurt her badly. He would feel the same way if the situations were reversed. But her family had been nothing like his. Would she have understood what he'd gone through?

As they entered the dining room, Jackson scanned the table. Discreet name cards marked where each person was to sit. He and Kristin were seated together, he noted. While being in such close proximity to her would play havoc on his senses, he could handle it, he told himself. And, on the bright side, he wouldn't be facing her, staring into those cold, angry gray eyes over the meal. Eyes he remembered more vividly being clouded with desire and satisfaction when they'd made love, or alight with intelligence and vivacity as they'd discussed their lectures.

They'd both majored in economics, with Kristin doing additional papers in business management and him in psychology. His choices had been driven by his need for independence from his family, and a last-ditch attempt to understand what it was that made his parents' relationship so dysfunctional. Kristin had told him very little about her family but he'd understood how close they were. He'd decided she would never be able to understand the twisted dynamics of his life and he'd never bothered trying to explain them, either.

Jackson stepped forward to pull out Kristin's chair for her, still deep in thought. In retrospect, knowing what he'd recently learned about Kristin's father, Douglas Richmond, and his double life, maybe she'd have a better understanding now.

"I can manage for myself," she snapped as she sat on her chair and pulled it in to the table herself.

And then again, maybe understanding wasn't her strongest suit right now, he conceded wryly. Nancy shot her daughter another one of those "mom looks" that made it clear her behavior was unacceptable. But Kristin remained defiant, deliberately turning her head to her brother Logan, who was seated on her other side, and acting as if Jackson wasn't even there.

Over the first course, Nancy directed her attention to him. "Tell us, Jackson, where have you been practicing until now?"

He smiled at Nancy and ignored the way Kristin stiffened next to him. She was trying so hard not to touch him it would have made him chuckle and call her on it if she hadn't made her antipathy toward him so obvious already. Even though he'd only just met the rest of the family, he'd felt their acceptance of his presence. And since he already had nothing but the utmost respect for Hector, he was determined to make this work.

"After I graduated I worked in litigation in California. I made a shift to general law several months ago, after taking a year off. When Hector made me his offer, I couldn't refuse."

"A year off? That was rather indulgent of you. It's a long time to be out of the loop." Kristin asked pointedly.

"It was necessary."

He could have gone into specifics but he was well used to keeping his personal life private; and the thought of discussing the last, distressing months of his late wife's life, together with his own recovery and grieving process after her loss, was abhorrent. Hector knew, and that was all that mattered to Jack. Hector and Jackson's late wife, Annie, had been at law school together and remained friends over many years. Yes, that meant he'd married a woman old enough to be his mother, but he wasn't about to make explanations here and now. Aside from the fact that her loss was still a raw wound in his heart, it was his business and his alone. And, more importantly, it wouldn't affect his ability to do his best for this family on legal matters.

A difficult silence spread across the table. One that Hector hastened to fill.

"Jackson was the first person I thought of when I realized I was ready to retire. We have been good friends for a long time and I both respect him and trust him implicitly. And I knew he was more than ready for a change of scenery. You'll be in excellent hands."

"He may have excellent hands," Kristin said provocatively, "but trust needs to be earned."

"I'm for accepting people at face value until proved otherwise," Logan interjected. "And I'm happy to accept Hector's recommendation. Jackson, thank you for taking us on. As you can see, we're a bit of a mixed bunch of personalities."

"Speak for yourself," Keaton said with a laugh. "Seriously, though, Jackson. We're glad that if we have to lose Hector as our attorney, he could recommend someone as highly as he speaks of you."

Jackson inclined his head in acknowledgement. To

his relief, as the first course finished and the second was brought to the table, conversation turned to more general topics, and he was able to sit back and listen to others talk. The dynamics of the family interested him. While the twins certainly looked identical, they were very different kinds of men. Hector had told him about Logan's background, that he'd been abducted as a baby and had only discovered his true identity a little over a year ago. He wondered if that made him still a bit of an outsider with Kristin and her other brother, Keaton.

He knew what it felt like to be an outsider in your own family. An only child of parents who were alternately viciously fighting or passionately absorbed in each other, he'd understood from an early age he was merely a peripheral accessory in his parents' lives. It had made him a loner growing up, slow to make friends. But despite his determination not to get into a romantic relationship while at college, Kristin's vibrancy and her intelligence, not to mention her looks, appealed to him on every level and he hadn't been able to resist asking her out. One date had led to several, despite her father's edict that she not date while she was in college, and before they knew it they were secretly living together. He'd always wondered what her dad was like—especially how he expected his daughter to focus solely on her studies at the exclusion of everything and everyone else. And, despite knowing from the outset they were from different worlds, he hadn't been able to resist the flame that was Kristin Richmond, when he'd met her. At least until the day his world had crashed through their bubble of joy and he'd walked away and never looked back.

"Jackson?" Tami, Keaton's partner, interrupted his thoughts.

"Sorry, I was miles away there. What did you say?"

Kristin flung him a look. "Goodness, Mr. Jones. If you can't even follow dinner conversation, how on earth can we trust you to handle our family's legal affairs?"

She'd commented lightly and with an entirely fake smile, but he hadn't missed the emphasis on the word *trust*. He had a lot of work to do.

"Kristin, you're being too harsh. You all can be overwhelming to newcomers, at first. Jackson, I was asking what you like to do in your spare time." Tami said with a friendly smile.

Jackson focused his attention on her. It was easier than acknowledging the prickly atmosphere that surrounded his neighbor at the table.

"I like hiking, sometimes on overnight treks, sometimes longer."

"So, not a team player, then?" Kristin asked, archly.

"I can play nicely with others," he responded, fighting the urge to grit his teeth. He kept a smile on his face as he continued. "But when I have time to myself, I tend to prefer my own company at least some of the time. Doesn't everyone?"

He felt as if he'd scored an invisible goal as everyone around the table, bar Kristin, murmured their assent.

"Earlier this year we had staff team building retreats in Sedona. There are some beautiful trails through there and it's such a contrast to the Pacific Northwest," Keaton commented.

The conversation thankfully turned to the twins' and their partners' experiences in Sedona and the personal obstacles they'd overcome, and Jackson let the conversation wash over him and listened carefully as they explained how Richmond Developments had initially specialized in building new residential and business precincts but, since Logan's return, had also begun repurposing existing heritage structures into community-friendly hubs that integrated well into modern living. He made a point to inject a pertinent comment here and there, if only to prove to the woman beside him that he really was paying attention. By the time dessert was served and eaten he felt as exhausted as though he'd run a marathon. While the food had no doubt been delicious, as well as artistically presented, he couldn't have told anyone what he'd eaten or what it had tasted like. But he could tell you exactly how the fragrance Kristin Richmond wore smelled.

She'd barely eaten anything during the course of the evening but had refilled her glass several times. As they stood to leave the dining table she swayed a little. He was quick to put a hand to her elbow to steady her. As expected, she tugged herself free.

"I'm fine," she muttered. "I don't need you pawing me."

"Good to know," he answered as neutrally as he could.

Her attitude was seriously grinding his gears. They needed to talk and clear the air. He was a professional and had put their past aside. He needed to know she could, too, which meant making a genuine apology and hopefully wiping the slate clear so he could continue to do his job. When Hector had offered him the opportunity to move to Seattle, he'd left everything behind in California—he needed to make things work here, because, when push came to shove, no matter what decisions he'd made, or when he'd made them, work was pretty much the only thing he had left. He would protect his ability to do his job to the best of his proficiency with whatever it took. Drunk ex-girlfriends notwithstanding.

"Kristin, darling. Are you feeling all right?" Nancy asked as they walked toward the large sitting room where the evening had begun.

"To be honest, Mom, I'm not feeling all that great. I think I just need a good night's sleep. I'll call my ride and head home, okay?"

"I'll take you home," Jackson heard himself saying.

What the hell? Where had that moment of chivalry come from? Yes, he knew he needed to make an apology to Kristin and to clear the air between them, but tonight was probably not the best time to do so. It appeared she felt the same way, judging by the expression of incredulity on her face. Even then, she still looked beautiful, dammit. Jackson realized the others had gone into the sitting room, leaving them hovering outside.

"That's not nec—" Kristin started, but Nancy overrode her.

"Oh, Jackson, that is wonderfully kind of you. You'd really soothe this mother's concerns if you could see her home safely."

Kristin flung her mom an incredulous look. "Mom, you've just met him and you're prepared to let him see me home?"

"Don't be silly, darling. He's Hector's friend and colleague. Besides," Nancy added quietly, "it seems to me that you have some apologizing to do for your behavior tonight. The ride home will be the perfect opportunity for you to do it. I don't know what's gotten into you this evening but you're not yourself and I don't like it."

"It's okay, Mrs. Richmond—Nancy," he corrected himself. "I can understand Kristin's reluctance to trust. Your family has been through a great deal in the past year and if I'm to work successfully with all of you, I need to put in the effort to understand exactly where you're all coming from."

"You're too kind," Nancy said with a smile and a pat on his arm. "I'll have Martha get your coats while I get Kristin's bag. I'll be right back."

The second her mom was gone, Kristin turned on him, her voice seething with antipathy.

"I don't know what you think you're doing, Jackson Jones, but I'm not happy about this. Not one bit."

"I get it, you don't trust me. I can assure you I

won't try to put a hand, or any other body part, on you for the duration of our trip to your home." At the reminder of their body parts touching he felt an unwelcome twinge of desire before he quelled the sensation as quickly as it had arisen. He took a breath. "We do, however, need to talk. Although perhaps tonight isn't the best time for it."

"Oh, why? Do you think I've had too much to drink?"

"I think you're tired and emotional and that you need some space. Seeing each other has come as a shock to both of us." That was probably the understatement of the year. "I'll see you safely home and maybe we can touch base tomorrow, have breakfast somewhere together, or lunch? Set the record straight between us so we can move forward."

Heated color suffused her cheeks and her eyes glittered dangerously. "If you're implying I'm still stuck in the past—"

"Not at all. Clearly you've moved on. We both have. But just as clearly we have unresolved issues to put to bed."

Ouch, that was probably not the best phrase to have used. He couldn't understand why he was being such a verbal klutz. His training and life experience had taught him to be far better than that.

"Please, Kristin. Let me see you home and then tomorrow we'll talk. Properly."

"Fine," she responded through tight lips as Martha approached them with their coats and Nancy arrived with Kristin's bag. "But don't think that any amount of talking will change the way I feel about you or your ability to represent my family."

"Noted," he said before turning to smile at the other women as they handed them their things.

"I've made your apologies to the others," Nancy said smoothly as she helped Kristin on with her coat. "They all send their best. And Jackson, we look forward to seeing more of you in the coming weeks."

"Thank you for a delightful evening," he said smoothly, ignoring the slight snort from Kristin.

"Good night, Mom. Thanks for dinner," Kristin said, leaning forward to hug her mom and kiss her on the cheek.

"And really rest up this weekend, hmm? No work, promise me?"

"No promises but I will take care of myself. And, Mom? I'm really glad for you and Hector."

"Thank you, that means a lot to me. Now, you two had better be off. There's more rain forecast tonight, so take care on the roads."

Jackson watched the interplay between mother and daughter, recognizing their closeness, and a part of him became wistful for something he'd never truly had. He might have let Kristin down all those years ago, but she'd had the support of her family, and still did. Whereas, right now, he had little but his home and his business. And that was just as he wanted it.

Wasn't it?

Three

Kristin sat in the soft leather passenger seat and stared straight out the windshield. Rain slanted across the glass, wiped rhythmically away by wiper blades as they cruised along the slick streets toward her apartment building in Mt. Baker. Jackson was a good driver, his broad, long-fingered hands sure on the wheel, and she found herself being lulled to sleep as they cruised on Interstate 90 over Lake Washington, only to jolt awake as Jackson spoke.

"Thank you for allowing me to see you home," he started as if choosing his words carefully.

"You're welcome. You've saved me a fare."

She was prepared to be charitable. Slightly.

"You always were good at making a dollar go farther than the average student," he said with a chuckle.

"I'm surprised you even remember that fact," she replied waspishly.

"I remember a lot of things. That's why I wanted to spend some time with you alone. To apologize."

She yawned widely and snuggled more comfortably in the seat. "Not now, Jackson. I'm not in the mood."

"Okay, fine. How about breakfast tomorrow?" he suggested.

"I plan to sleep in…late."

"Lunch?"

"Might indulge in a round of golf," she said, starting to enjoy this more than she expected.

Of course, she'd never swung a club in her life, nor did she have any idea if greens were open at this time of year, but it sounded important. Certainly more important than listening to the excuses of a man who had walked out on her and their dreams for a future together.

"Brunch, then. I'll pick you up at ten."

"I'll probably still be sleeping."

"Well, then, I'll wake you up. I can be quite persuasive."

He left his comment hanging in the air like a memory from a long-ago moment. Kristin couldn't help it. Her body tensed as she remembered exactly how persuasive he could be first thing in the morning and how often she'd been late for an early lecture because of it. Thank goodness they were nearly at her turnoff.

"Look, what happened in the past has no bearing

on now. We've both moved on. I don't know what your reasons were for abandoning me then, and, I don't care anymore because you showed your true colors when you left without a care for my feelings or the relationship we'd had. Based on that, I can only surmise that you're unreliable and therefore totally unsuited to represent my family in our legal affairs. I don't see how an apology now will change that."

"You always were intractable," he commented. "I'm sorry, I shouldn't have said that. But I agree with you. We have both moved on. Allow me an opportunity to prove to you that I'm the right person to handle your family's legal affairs. If, after a fair trial, you still feel I'm not the person for you, then perhaps one of the other attorneys at Ramirez Law would be a better fit."

Ire rose hot and thick in her throat, choking her with its bitterness. She swallowed against it and forced herself to calm down. When she spoke, it was with icy precision.

"Adult? You think if I don't just accept your re-entry into my life I'm being childish? Don't you dare begin to presume you know me. You may have thought you did, once, but you proved you really had no idea of who I was or what your leaving would do to me. You can pull over here. This is my building."

The minute his car stopped in the drop-off zone, she pushed open her door and got out, her heels clicking sharply as she marched toward the main doors. She heard his car door slam shut behind her, followed by steps that closed in quickly.

"I can see myself in, thank you."

"I promised Nancy I would see you safely home. Call me old-fashioned, but that means seeing a lady to her door."

"Oh, I could call you a lot of things. Old-fashioned definitely isn't one of them. And you needn't bother. My building has security."

He put a hand to her elbow and stopped her mid-stride. "Kristin, please. Let me honor my promise to your mom."

"Like you honored your promises to me eleven years ago? I don't think so."

She freed herself from his touch and scanned her entry card to the building. "Please go, or I will call security to remove you."

Kristin let herself in through the door and swiftly crossed the foyer to the elevator bank where she swiped her card again. As the doors opened, she stepped inside and turned around. Jackson stood on the other side of the main doors to the building, watching her every move. As the elevator doors began to slide closed, he gave her a short salute. She turned away, but the image of him was burned on her memory. And not only the image he'd left just now. No, there were more—so many more. Jackson stepping out of the shower with rivulets of water pouring off his lean, strong body. Jackson making love to her, long and slow on a Sunday morning. Jackson laughing at something she'd said, or done. So many memories.

And he'd walked away from all of them, she reminded himself sternly. The elevator stopped at her floor, and she walked to her corner apartment, fighting the burn of tears. She would not let them fall. She'd promised herself years ago she would never waste another drop of emotion on Jackson Jones. And she wouldn't. Not even anger. Not anymore.

The shock of seeing him tonight had taught her that her feelings for him and her hurt over the way he'd treated her still lingered. Reacting to him as she had tonight was childish. She knew that. Accepted it. And now she moved on.

Kristin dragged in a long breath and blew it out slowly. From this point on, she would be zen about Jackson Jones. That didn't mean she had to trust him, but she wouldn't give him the satisfaction of getting under her skin again. She'd said what she had to say tonight. He knew where he stood.

She was conflicted. A part of her wanted to tell her family that eleven years ago he'd dumped her and run, and to kick him to the curb. But then she'd have to admit that she hadn't exactly held up her end of her deal with her father about her college education by having had a relationship. And then there was the professional relationship between Hector and Jack. She had a wealth of respect for her mom's fiancée. He wouldn't do anything to jeopardize her family.

She chewed her lower lip a moment and came to her decision. She'd give Jack that trial period, maybe a month was reasonable, and he would need to work darn hard if he was going to successfully prove his suitability as their family attorney.

She got ready for bed and stood at her window, staring out toward Lake Washington. Tomorrow was a new day, and she'd tackle it the way she'd tackled everything else in her life. Head-on and full of vigor.

Head-on and full of vigor hadn't counted on the hangover Kristin had woken with at 5:00 a.m. Unable to continue to sleep, she'd downed several large glasses of water and decided to get dressed and head into the office. Of course there was the small matter of not having her car but she called a service and arranged for a driver to collect her at 6:30 a.m. With any luck she'd be able to power through the balance of the work she hadn't finished last night thanks to her mom's summons for dinner.

Last night would have been a delightful family celebration if it hadn't been for the arrival of Jackson Jones. No, she corrected herself, her lips twisting slightly as she eyed her reflection in the mirror. *She* had been the fly in the ointment last night. Her behavior had undoubtedly upset her mom, and Kristin owed her an apology— and her sincere congratulations on Nancy and Hector's plans for their future. She made a mental note to send her mom and Hector a gift basket to celebrate their good news and set a reminder in her phone to call her mom to make the necessary apology and possibly mention that she and Jack hadn't exactly parted friends. Although, knowing her mom, that might open a can of worms on a past she had put firmly behind her. Maybe she just needed to suck it up.

Her phone beeped a five-minute warning for her ride. Her stomach burned, making her reach for an apple from her fruit bowl before she exited her apartment. Not the most filling of breakfasts, but it would do.

She'd been working steadily, cross-checking data reports her secretary had prepared for her last week, when her cell phone buzzed on her desk. She looked up in irritation. The headache that played behind her right eye due to her overindulgence last night intensified as she stared at the screen. A private number. She flicked it to voice mail and carried on working, but the screen lit up again. She ignored it and had just settled into the patterns of the numbers she was reviewing when her desk phone rang. The only people who used her direct line were either staff, her immediate family, who wouldn't have been calling the office today, or security downstairs. She hit the speaker button.

"This is Kristin Richmond," she said far more crisply than she felt.

"Sorry to bother you, Ms. Richmond. It's Tower security. I have a man here who insists he has an appointment with you."

A prickle of warning ran along Kristin's nape.

"An appointment?"

"He asked me to let you know he's brought brunch. His name is Jackson Jones."

Her stomach growled, assuring her that the apple she'd half consumed a few hours ago was entirely insufficient for a woman with a hangover.

She sighed. Clearly Jackson had not developed the knack of taking a hint. An imp of mischief urged her to tell the guard to send the food up but leave the man behind, but she'd agreed, with herself at least, to be adult about this.

"Fine. Send him up. Oh, and add him to the approved visitor list, too, please. From Monday we'll be seeing a lot more of him here, I expect. He's taking over from Mr. Ramirez for my family. For now, at least."

Kristin walked through the empty office to the elevator lobby and waited for Jackson to arrive. She didn't have to wait long. As the elevator pinged, she felt a shimmer of anticipation combined with a liberal dose of nerves. She had been insufferably rude last night, and in doing so, she'd ended up giving him the power in their relationship—if you could call it such a thing. She was going to be cool and professional, and set a standard for them to move forward. She didn't have to like him working for the family, but his true colors would show, and he'd be dismissed when that happened.

Jackson exited the elevator with a sure stride, a brown paper bag swinging from one hand and two disposable coffee cups in a holder in the other. Extra-large coffee cups, she noted with approval. He was dressed casually, in jeans, boots and a knit sweater with a well-worn leather jacket over the top. His hair was mussed and slightly wet from the weather outdoors. Dammit, he looked incredible. The years since she'd last seen him had only served to make him even more attractive than he'd been in his early twenties and her stupid heart did a ridiculous pitter-patter in response.

"You're persistent," she said, suddenly feeling awkward.

"I'll bet you didn't eat this morning."

"I'll have you know I had an apple. And what's it to you? I already have one mother, I don't need a second." She closed her eyes and took a leveling breath. "I'm sorry. I told myself I would behave today."

"Behave?" Humor lit his blue eyes with a wicked gleam. "Are you sure you're Kristin Richmond?"

She couldn't help it—she cracked a grin. "Funny guy. Now pass me my coffee."

"Yours is the one on the right. Hazelnut skinny latte—I took a guess that you haven't changed the way you take it."

She carefully extricated the cup from the holder and took a sip. The hot liquid scalded her mouth, but the flavor exploded on her tongue with a welcome charge of energy.

"It's perfect," she said. "Now, what did you bring to eat?"

"Bacon-and-egg breakfast bagels. I figured you'd need the carbs after last night."

She narrowed her gaze at him. "A gentleman wouldn't feel the need to mention last night. Or how I might be feeling this morning."

"No one ever accused me of being a gentleman."

She snorted in agreement. "Follow me. We can eat in my office."

He did as she suggested. With every step, she was aware of his body close behind hers. When they reached her office, she gestured to the visitor couches.

"I'll grab some napkins," she said.

"No bother, I have everything we need."

A little flustered with nothing else to do but sit and face him, Kristin occupied herself with taking another gulp of her coffee. As the caffeine hit her system, she realized she was starting to feel almost human. Jackson showed no such signs of discomfort and set out their wrapped bagels and napkins on the coffee table between them.

"Two bagels and an order of hash browns?" she commented.

"The hash browns are yours. I figured you'd be hungry. You barely ate last night. And I remember how feral you used to get when you didn't eat properly."

And what else did he remember? she wondered. Did he remember how they used to cuddle in bed, sated after making love? Did he remember the long walks they took discussing the lectures they'd sat through and arguing the various case studies they'd observed? Did he remember telling her he loved her and wanted to be with her forever?

Kristin slammed a metaphorical gate closed on that thinking. It would get her nowhere. She focused instead on the emptiness she'd felt when she returned to the miserably small apartment they'd shared, and known, the instant she'd set foot through the front door, that he was gone. She'd hunted high and low for a note of some kind that would explain where he was and when he'd return. She'd phoned and messaged him and their friends more times than she could count. And she'd received nothing in return. Nothing but emptiness and heartache.

She wasn't going to dwell on the past. After the shock of seeing him last night, and in the cold light of day this morning, she'd decided she was going to rise above it. Of course he still had to prove he was worthy of her family's trust. And while she was happy to accept food, she wasn't going to make things easy for him. That said, she owed him an apology.

"Before we eat, I just wanted to say sorry for being rude to you last night. I shouldn't have let my personal feelings spoil what was supposed to be a happy occasion for my mom and Hector or what was supposed to be a civil introduction to you."

He looked at her and didn't speak for a moment. She saw a pulse flicker near his right eye. A tell she hadn't realized she was searching for until she saw it. He might look cool, calm and collected, but this was hitting him on an emotional level.

"Thank you," he said heavily. "And I, too, owe you an apology for the way I left you. I had—"

"Water under the bridge," she said succinctly, reached for a wrapped bagel and made a big deal out of opening it. Before taking a bite, though, she looked across at him. "I'm still not sold on you being our attorney, though. Just so you understand. Apologies aside, I don't trust you not to let us down."

He nodded slowly. "Noted."

She took a bite of her bagel and moaned in delight. "Oh, this is so good."

They ate in companionable silence and, without even the slightest embarrassment, Kristin finished her coffee and consumed her food like a woman starved. She wiped her fingers on a paper napkin and stowed their trash in the carry bag to dispose of later.

"Look, thanks for bringing brunch, but I need you to leave now," she said bluntly. Now that her blood sugars were zinging along as normal and her equilibrium was restored, she felt more confident. "I have a lot of work to get through before a presentation to the finance committee on Monday."

"I'd hoped we could talk. Really talk."

"Is that necessary? I've apologized. You've apologized. We've broken bread together, or bagels anyway. Let's just move on, okay?"

"Whatever the lady wants," he said with a wry twist to his lips.

What the lady wanted was answers but she'd be damned first before asking for them. History had taught her that all she'd hear was excuses, or lies, and she really wasn't in the mood for them. Not now, not ever.

"Look, no one in my family knows what we meant to each other before." *If I even actually meant anything to you*, she added silently. "And they don't need to know. I'd be happiest if we could just move on as old college acquaintances touching base for the first time in a long time."

"Won't they have questions after last night?"

"After my performance, you mean?"

He quirked a half smile and nodded.

"I'll sort that out," she replied.

And she would. She'd tell her mom that she and Jackson had had a difference of opinion that had never been resolved. It wasn't so far from the truth. She'd also make it clear that she didn't want to talk about it and that they had reached an amicable agreement about leaving the past where it belonged.

"You always could be persuasive," he said with another of those half smiles.

She wished he'd stop doing that. Referencing their history and smiling that smile that had always melted her resolve. It reminded her of better times together. Happier times. Times before the world went crazy, along with everyone in it. But then, experience had shown her that was life. You had to roll with it, dodge what you could and take the hits when you couldn't. By now, she ought to be an expert, right?

She stood and looked pointedly at him, expecting him to do the same.

"Let me walk you to the lobby," she said.

He stood and continued to face her. "It's okay. I'll see myself out. I appreciate you making time for me. I half expected you to say you'd take the food but refuse to see me."

"That was my first reaction when I heard you were downstairs," she admitted with a rueful laugh. "But we have a truce now, right?"

"A truce," he agreed.

He put out his hand and maintained steady eye contact with her, challenging her to shake it. Kristin lifted her chin slightly and put her hand in his, fighting the sensations that threatened to rob her of breath as they touched. His skin was warm and smooth. His grip firm but gentle. It didn't take a stretch of the imagination to remember what that hand had felt like caressing her body, her breasts, her thighs. That intimate connection was still there. Still overwhelming. It took every ounce of control she possessed to allow him to shake her hand and not to yank hers free the moment she possibly could. And yet, when he let her hand go, she felt oddly bereft.

"Right, now that's settled, I'll get back to work," she said brusquely. "Have a good weekend."

"You, too," he said. "It was good to talk."

She watched as he turned and left, heading back the way she'd brought him. Even dressed as casually as he was, he was a commanding presence. He'd always had that about him. The ability to draw the eye and the attention of anyone in the vicinity. Kristin shook her head slightly, as if to rid herself of the image, and turned back to her desk.

Suddenly the idea of studying reports and figures and facts in preparation for her presentation on Monday held no appeal, but she'd do it. Because that was what she did. She got on with things. No matter how much she'd rather be doing something else and no matter how much it hurt.

Four

On Monday morning, Jackson settled in his office chair and studied the mail his assistant had brought him.

Jackson had spent half the weekend here, taking a leaf out of Kristin's book, and he finally had a better handle on what to expect from the Richmond family, among other clients. They'd certainly been through a lot, what with the death of the patriarch of the family, Douglas Richmond, and the subsequent discovery of an entire new branch of the family, swiftly followed by the corporate espionage issue.

He had to take his hat off to both sets of the siblings for the way they'd managed to engineer an amicable solution between them. It had not only drawn them closer as brothers and sisters but also strengthened their businesses as they worked together on specific projects at the same time. The file mentioned the half siblings in Virginia—Fletcher, Mathias and Lisa. He honestly didn't understand how Douglas Richmond could have done it—established two separate families on opposite coasts and lived happily with each of them without the other ever finding out until he died. And yet, from what Hector had told him, despite everything their father had done, the children seemed to have taken it all in their stride and were working hard to remain united as a family.

Jackson leaned back a little more and, resting his elbows on the arms of his chair, steepled his fingers. How different would his life have been, he wondered, if he'd had siblings to share the burdens? He huffed out a breath and let his hands drop to his desk. There was no point in speculating. His life was what it was. The choices he'd made, the people he'd hurt, that was what he had to live with. At least he'd gotten one thing right.

He looked across his desk to the photo of his late wife and felt that all too raw, familiar tug of loss. He picked up the frame and traced her cheek with the tip of one finger. After Kristin he hadn't wanted to love again. Losing someone simply hurt too much. But his love for Annie had snuck under his safeguards, and she had become everything to him. Mentor, lover, friend, wife. Theirs hadn't been a traditional relationship in any way, shape or form, but he had loved her with everything in him. She was the first and only person he'd ever spoken to about his parents and their twisted relationship—and about their deaths. She'd offered him compassion and encouraged him to seek help understanding how their choices had affected him. Her quiet support had been immeasurable and there were days he missed her with a wholehearted ache that took his breath away.

It was over a year since her shock diagnosis of stage four kidney cancer. He'd stopped work immediately to nurse her through the pain and nausea. Watching her grow weaker and weaker had only made him love her and her resilient spirit even more. When she'd passed only three months later, it was as if a light had been extinguished in his life. He'd needed time to come to terms with her loss and his life without her in it. Hector's approach a couple of months ago had been the impetus he'd needed to grasp life with both hands again—and it helped him to honor the final promise he'd made to Annie. But would he have taken the lifeline quite so keenly had he known Kristin Richmond was part of it?

Leaving her the way he had, so long ago, had been the deepest regret of his life. Back then he hadn't seen any other way. His life had suddenly and irrevocably imploded. The scandal and unwelcome publicity revolving around his parents' sudden deaths would have been an unfair test of his and Kristin's relationship. So he'd made a split-second decision to sever ties without looking back. It was easier not to have to make any explanations—just simply leave. Easier in physical terms, if not emotional ones.

And now, of course, he was reaping the damage of

his twenty-one-year-old brain's decision, and he had to prove to her he could be trusted to handle her family's affairs. If the situations were reversed, would he be ready to trust the person who'd walked out without a backward glance? No, he couldn't blame her for her reaction, especially when her family had already been through so much. But Hector had put his trust in him and he owed it to the older man to stick with this even if it was uncomfortable. As Annie had always said, nothing worthwhile came easy. Building trust with Kristin would have to be a careful process and he knew it wouldn't be a simple task.

There was a noise at the door as his assistant came into his office with a messenger bag in her hand.

"This arrived for you," she said, handing the packet over to him. She noted the photo still in his hands. "Nice picture. Your mom?"

"No, she was my wife."

He didn't blame her for the assumption. Annie had indeed been old enough to be his mom, but he also wished that, just for once, people wouldn't make the automatic assumption and judge her or their relationship based on their ages.

His assistant's eyes widened, and her cheeks pinkened. "I'm so sorry. I didn't mean any offense."

"None taken. Please, don't worry about it."

She nodded and left his office, closing the door behind her as she went. Jackson studied the messenger bag, surprised to see how it had been addressed. *To the Attorney representing Douglas Richmond's Estate.* He turned it over in his hand. The return address was a mailing office in Tacoma with no hint as to who had sent it. He reached for the letter opener on his desk and neatly slit the bag open.

There was a single sheet inside, and he opened it carefully, laying it flat on his desk as he started to read.

I wish to make a claim against the estate of the late Douglas Richmond on the basis that I am one of his children. Douglas Richmond and my mother had an affair twenty-five years ago, while she was working for him, and I was the result. He made a large severance payment to her on the basis that she say nothing to anyone about my existence.

My mother recently passed away, and I found evidence of this payment to her along with a letter outlining the conditions for her acceptance of it. I am convinced that I have the right to be recognized as one of Mr. Richmond's children. I have the right to an equal portion of any monies that are being distributed to his heirs.

I do recognize that my existence may come as a shock to the family and I am prepared to keep my details and my claim private provided that I receive a sum of money equivalent to what would have been my share by January, one calendar month and one day from the date of this letter. If I receive that money, I will, like my mother, sign a hush statement and take the secret of my paternal identity to the grave.

However, if you do not give my claim the seriousness it deserves, I will not hesitate to take my story to the media. I am sure you are aware of the Richmond family's need for privacy and stability at this time—more media scrutiny would be damaging to their reputation and their company position—so I expect to hear from you within the next week via the below email address.

Jackson read the note a second time and mentally debated the veracity of the claim. The not-so-subtle implication of taking the story to the media was a big red flag for him. Extortion was never pretty and the police would have to be involved if the Richmonds agreed. If the author of the letter was indeed a child of Douglas Richmond, then surely they could have simply fronted up and made their claim legally. Either way, the threat was clearly stated. If the family didn't accede to the claimant's wishes, they would go to the media. Jackson had a duty of care to the family, and that meant updating them and Hector about this development as soon as possible.

He carefully crafted an email to both sides of the Richmond family as well as Hector and the lawyer representing the Virginia side of the family, inviting them to an urgent video conference with him later that day. Over the course of the morning, the responses came in. A negative from the woman who had incorrectly claimed to be Douglas's legitimate first wife, Eleanor Richmond in Virginia, and an apology from her daughter, Lisa, citing a preexisting appointment she couldn't shift. From the brothers and Nancy, Hector and the other lawyer there were affirmatives, but from Kristin there was nothing.

Jackson looked at the time on his computer. There was still time for her to respond. He set himself to attending to the rest of his day. The Richmonds, as much as they were a major client, were not his only client.

The day passed swiftly, and the time for the video conference arrived. Still no word from Kristin, but that didn't mean she wouldn't appear on his screen along with everyone else. Jackson opened the video conference and waited for everyone to virtually arrive. Everyone who'd RSVP'd appeared within a few minutes, but there was no sign of Kristin.

"Hi everyone," he said with a nod to his screen. "I'm glad so many of you could make it today, and Fletcher and Mathias, with the time difference I'm glad you could attend. I have received some disturbing correspondence that I need to share with you. I'll scan and forward it to you by email after this meeting, but for now, I wanted to read the content to you myself."

The others remained silent while he read the letter he'd received that morning out to them. There was a stunned silence for about three seconds after he'd finished, and then the expressions of disgust and shock began. Mathias was the most vocal.

"Who is this person? How can we trust they're telling the truth? It all sounds a little far-fetched to me.

While it's true Dad may have had an affair, for him to hush things up like that doesn't sound right. He may have been a bigamist but he provided for all of us as he obviously did for this person's mother, too, if their story is to be believed. This sounds to me like someone thinks we'll be an easy touch for the money."

There was wry agreement from Keaton and Fletcher. Nancy cleared her throat and leaned closer to her screen.

"Do you think their threat to go to the media is a credible one? We can't afford another scandal, not on top of how hard it was to recover from losing customer confidence after Douglas's duplicity and the subsequent espionage attack on our business. Together with the global recession and recovery, we don't need any more adverse publicity," she said firmly.

Logan nodded. "My thoughts exactly, Mom. What do you propose we do, Jackson? We can't really afford to call their bluff and ignore their demand. Do we even know who this person is?"

"No, we have no identifying information at this time, but obviously if they expect us to take them seriously they will have to provide documents—the hush agreement they reference in the letter, as well as birth certificates and photo ID. I suggest we ask for such information before we agree to proceed any further. They will need to prove their claim and provide DNA samples." He sighed. "This does sound like extortion and people like this are tenacious. Whether their claim is genuine or not, they will doggedly hold out to get their money, what they see as their due, one way or another."

"One way or another?" Fletcher asked. "You're referring to what a media outlet might pay for an exclusive, right? Can't we do something with gag orders?"

"That's probably premature at this stage and first we need to know who they are. When I request the necessary proof they might back down, but something tells me they're not that kind of person. And we may need to involve the police."

"No police. Not until we know if they're genuinely a member of this family. You and Hector will have your work cut out with this," Nancy said,

"Of course," Hector interjected. "I was your family attorney at the time this person asserts their mother had an affair with Douglas. I know I never received instruction from him about this."

"Nor I," said the attorney for the Virginia family.

Nancy shook her head. "I feel sure that I would have noticed if he had an affair right under my nose here in the office, but he fooled me for years with Eleanor and the rest of you kids, so I can't trust my own judgment anymore."

"That's totally understandable and you are not to blame here, Nancy," Jackson said firmly. "We will get to the bottom of this. Fletcher, Mathias, can I ask you to let your mother and sister know what is happening?"

They both affirmed in the positive.

Keaton spoke up again then. "I'll talk to Kristin.

I don't know what kept her from attending. I believe her presentation finished an hour ago."

"Perhaps she didn't receive the email in time," Jackson replied. "But if you could get her up to speed, I'd appreciate it."

Everyone signed off from the video conference, and Jackson was left staring at his blank screen. Was Kristin simply too busy to have read her email, or had she seen it and decided against responding because, apology or no apology, she still harbored a grudge against him?

They really needed to clear the air properly. A hurried breakfast of bagels and coffee last Saturday hadn't allowed him to say any of the things he knew he needed to tell her even if she'd been ready to listen. And while she'd apologized for being rude to him, she'd made it quite clear she still didn't trust him. It was going to make working with her exceptionally difficult if this continued, and wouldn't reflect well on either of them.

He didn't want to let the family down, nor Hector, who'd had faith in him and placed the practice in his hands. Too much hinged on what had happened between Kristin and Jackson in the past. He needed to see it brought out into the open, every last hideous detail, and dealt with so they could work together effectively. Because if she had no idea why he'd had to leave her so abruptly eleven years ago, how could he expect her to trust him now, when it was vital the family all drew together?

Five

Kristin looked up at the knock on her office door and smiled as she saw Keaton stroll in and sit down opposite her desk.

"Hello, brother. How're you doing?" she asked, putting down her pen and pushing her papers to one side so she could give him her full attention.

"Pretty good, considering."

"Considering?"

"Considering what?"

"That there's another potential sibling of ours out there, and they want their cut of the pie that makes up Dad's estate."

"You're kidding me, right?"

There was nothing teasing in the look on Keaton's

face, and he simply shook his head in response to her incredulous reply.

"When did you find out?" she demanded. "What's going on?"

"That's what we're all hoping to find out, soon," he replied.

"What do you mean, we?"

"Me, Mom, Logan, Fletcher, Mathias. I expect Eleanor and Lisa also know by now."

"Hang on, why am I not included in this family list?" she demanded.

A legal claim against the family? This had to have come via Jackson, surely. Why hadn't he seen fit to tell her about it? Was this some kind of petty revenge against her for her behavior last Friday night? She'd apologized—reservedly, sure—but she'd had the impression they were going forward with a clean slate. A sudden rage built up inside her and threatened to boil over in a stream of incredibly unladylike language. How dare he do this to her? Cut her out of her own family business? The sooner he was replaced, the better.

"Before you get yourself all worked up and mad at the wrong people or person, tell me if you've checked your email since this morning," Keaton said in an irritatingly placatory tone.

"Of course I checked my email," she snapped. "I check hourly for important correspondence."

"So you received the group mail from Jackson this morning?"

She thought back. Yes, she had received it,

skimmed the subject header with its summons to a video conference and decided she was too busy to attend. Too busy to even let him know, to be honest. And she'd deleted the email, unread.

"I did, yes." It wasn't exactly a lie.

"Did you read it?"

"Of course I did," she said defiantly. She *had* read the header and known she had too many other demands on her time to join the meeting.

"Then you decided an urgent call to action was beneath you when we were all involved?" Keaton pressed relentlessly.

"Keaton, you know what my days are like since Isaac left. Who has time to read the contents of every single email that comes into their inbox?"

"Ah, yes, Isaac. Seems to me that looking for his replacement should be at the top of your to-do list."

"It's not that easy. I have to be able to trust whoever takes his place. They have to be thoroughly vetted—not only by HR but by me—and that takes time I don't have at the moment."

"I know, I know, we're all time-poor and even lower on trust when it comes to newcomers. The espionage business really did a number on all of us. Did Tami tell you more charges have been laid against her father?"

Kristin shook her head. Tami had cut herself off from her parents when she was eighteen, but when she'd needed his help, her dad, Warren Everard, had tried to use her to infiltrate his biggest business rival, Richmond Developments. He'd had spies planted throughout the Richmond team. Spies like Isaac, who'd been flushed out after a thorough internal investigation.

Keaton waved a hand, dismissing that train of thought. "That's not what I'm here about. It's this new claim on Dad's estate."

He spent the next few minutes summarizing the meeting with Jackson and what they'd agreed would happen next.

"So you didn't really need me there anyway," she said in an attempt to excuse herself. "Sounds as though you have it all sorted, for now anyway."

Keaton looked at her strangely. "To be honest, I'm surprised you weren't in there telling us all what to do. What gives between you and Jackson Jones? A man would have to be blind, deaf and dumb not to have noticed the tension between the two of you last Friday at Mom's."

She stiffened in her chair. "Look, I'm sorry if I made the evening awkward for you all. I was in a bad mood, and I shouldn't have taken it out on all of you."

"To be honest, you only took it out on one person. And a stranger to boot."

"He isn't a stranger. At least, not to me."

There, she'd admitted that she and Jackson had a past. By the look on Keaton's face, she knew she wasn't going to get out of this one lightly.

"Do I have to punch his face in?"

Kristin laughed, which was obviously what Keaton had intended all along, to lighten her mood, and she saw her brother's face relax.

"Maybe not this week. Seriously, though, we knew each other in college. Very well," she added in answer to his raised brow. "I thought we shared the same goals and dreams for a future together. I was wrong."

There, she'd managed to put it in a nutshell. Hopefully, Keaton would leave it at that.

"He hurt you badly, didn't he? Maybe I should just punch him for the hell of it."

She should've known her brother wouldn't let it go if he thought someone had hurt her. "Given his chosen profession, he'd probably sue," she said.

"Yeah, there is that. And the fact that he's working for us and from the way he's responded to the new claim, he appears competent. I guess I should just bide my time."

She gave him another smile.

"How's Tami coping with this business with her dad?"

"As well as can be expected. Even though they haven't spoken in months, she's still worried for him. Frankly, after the way he treated her, both recently and in the past, he's darn lucky she even acknowledges he's her father. Besides, with the work she's doing in conjunction with Mom and the Richmond Foundation, she's too busy to give him more than a cursory thought. And we have a wedding to plan, too."

"You're talking about Mom and Hector's wedding?"

"No, I'm talking about Tami's and my wedding," he said with a wide grin on his face.

"Oh my! That's fantastic news. I thought you two were taking it slow. Finding your feet together."

"We've found them, and we want to make it official. What can I say? I love the woman with all my heart and I want to be able to shout that out for all the world to hear."

Kristin eyed her brother with a touch of envy. He looked so very happy. After the turmoil of the past year, he deserved happiness; they all did. Logan and Honor were going to become parents. Mom and Hector were getting married soon, and now Keaton and Tami. Seemed like everyone who meant anything to her was pairing up and moving on, without her.

"Well, congratulations. When will you make an announcement?"

"We were thinking Christmas Eve for the family, and waiting till mid-January for the formal announcement. We don't want to steal any of Mom and Hector's thunder at their wedding. But I wanted you to know. You've been looking really stressed and unhappy lately and it's not like you. The unhappy part, anyway. Stress, well, you cope with that well enough under normal circumstances but things haven't been normal with our family for a long time now."

"True, and thanks for sharing your news with me. Does Tami know you were going to tell me?"

"Yeah, she's worried about you, too."

"That's sweet of her, of both of you, but there's nothing to worry about. Except maybe this potential new sibling. Do you think there's any basis to what they're claiming?"

"Who knows? With Dad, anything could be true.

I can't believe I'm saying that but since he died nothing seems to make a lot of sense anymore."

She snorted. "Yeah, I know what you mean."

They fell silent for a while before Keaton rose to his feet.

"I don't know about you," he said, "but some of us have work to do. Nice chatting."

She quirked a smile at him. "I'd like to remind you that I was the one working when you arrived here in my office to disrupt my train of thought."

"Well, you better get back on the train. Time's a-wasting."

With that he gave her a half-cocked grin and left. She sat for a while staring at the door he'd closed behind him. That was typical Keaton. Breeze in, deliver shocking news and breeze right on out leaving her to deal with it. Okay, so maybe that summary of facts wasn't entirely fair. They'd knocked heads over a lot of things here at Richmond Developments but for the most part they worked together well. Far better than they ever had as children.

Keaton had always been hell-bent on being the best at everything. Always trying to win their father's favor and prove that while his twin may have been missing since they were a day old, Keaton, the remaining son, was more than enough for the Richmond family. Logan's return had been a shock to everyone, but to Keaton most of all. Still, they'd all found their new normal. It just felt like hers was a lonely one.

Which brought her full circle to Jackson Jones.

She supposed she ought to reach out to him and get all the facts on this new threat to their family's security. Just as she reached for her phone, it rang.

"Kristin Richmond," she said crisply, reaching for her pen and a piece of paper to jot down notes should they be necessary.

"Kristin, it's Jack."

The hairs on her neck prickled in response to the deep timbre of his voice. Even though she'd just been thinking about him, it still came as a surprise to have him on the phone.

"I was about to call you. Keaton just filled me in on the new development."

"Good, good," he said. "I didn't want you to be the last to hear. It's a pity you couldn't make the video conference."

"Look, I'm sorry about that but I'm short-staffed and hard-pressed with budgets and end-of-year reports right now." And why the heck was she making excuses to him like this. He worked for her—well, her family not the other way around. "I wonder if you could give me your full version of events, just in case Keaton missed anything important."

"Sure," he agreed. He went through everything that had happened in chronological order, including the discussion during the video conference. "So, that's where we are. My assistant has emailed you a scan of the letter of claim together with a transcript of the video conference."

She nodded approvingly. He certainly was being efficient.

"Do you think the claim is authentic?" she asked.

"To be honest, if they were legitimate I would have expected them to approach me through their own legal counsel. That said, they may simply be unaware of what the process ought to be and, if they've only recently become party to the information they have shared with us, this could all be as much of a surprise to them as it is to us."

"But they're threatening to go to the media if we don't play ball," Kristin pointed out, not prepared to be magnanimous about this new situation. "And they're keeping their identity secret and not giving us all the documents up-front."

"Yes, there is that, and extortion is a crime, which I have pointed out to them in my reply."

"It seems like a heavy-handed tactic on their part. Surely, if they believe their claim is true, they would be reasonable about this."

"I would have thought so, which is why I suggested we tread carefully and make sure we have all the information we need before taking anything further," he said firmly.

"So, now we wait, yes?"

"I don't expect the claimant will delay responding to my request for more information. Now they've opened the door, I expect they'll want things to move quickly."

"Right, well, thank you. Is that everything you wanted to discuss?"

There was a slight hesitation at the end of the line before he spoke again. "Actually, there is something else we need to discuss. I have another client due shortly and I'm sure you're pressed for time, as well. Would you be free for dinner tonight?"

"Tonight?"

She scrambled in her mind for an excuse not to go, but she had no valid reason to refuse. And, after missing today's video conference, she owed it to him to accept. Besides which, her daytime calendar was packed with commitments, but her evenings stretched out emptily unless she stayed late in the office.

"Or tomorrow?" he pressed.

"No, no, tonight is fine. Where and when?"

He gave her details of a restaurant not too far from her apartment building and suggested seven o'clock.

"Sure, I'll be there," she said.

"Thanks, Kristin."

She started to say, "You're welcome," but he'd already disconnected the call. She put the receiver back in its cradle and stared at the phone. So, dinner tonight. She blew out a long breath. What did they need to discuss? She blinked and redirected her focus to the papers she'd put to one side when Keaton had arrived. No doubt she'd discover what Jackson wanted to talk about soon enough. In the meantime, she had to do the work of two people in half the time.

Kristin found it difficult to settle into the rhythm of her work. Her mind kept straying to the clock, checking to make sure she'd left sufficient time for herself to get home, get changed and get to the restaurant on time. In the end, she locked away her documents and shut down her laptop earlier than she'd planned. Somehow, Jackson Jones was still doing a number on her concentration, much like he had when they were in college. It felt like she couldn't move for thinking about him.

And she kept thinking about him. All through the drive home and all through the time she took to get ready for dinner. Even in the quick shower she'd taken to wash away the stress of her day, she couldn't get him out of her mind. As the deliciously hot water sluiced over her body, she couldn't help remembering what it had felt like to have his hands on her. Touching her—stroking, tweaking, probing.

She groaned with need as she stroked her body with a soapy bath sponge, lingering over the sensitive areas just that little longer. Teasing herself, but not allowing herself the respite she knew she could give with just the right amount of pressure. It was madness to do this, especially before going to meet Jackson. He left her on tenterhooks enough as it was.

She turned the faucet to a far cooler setting and let the water run over her before switching it off and drying herself rapidly. She hadn't bothered to wash her hair and twisted the length of it into a coil on top of her head. A few wisps of hair snuck out to kiss the side of her neck, sending a light shiver through her. She was so tightly wound she felt as though she'd snap under the right provocation.

Perhaps agreeing to see Jackson for dinner tonight had not been the best idea, but she couldn't back out now.

Kristin selected a plain black dress that settled around midthigh, skimming her curves nicely. She kept her makeup minimal but chose a vibrant red lipstick as a don't-mess-with-me statement. A chunky gold necklace was the perfect accessory at her throat, breaking the severity of the dress. Sheer black stockings and knee-high, heeled boots completed her ensemble. The ride she'd booked was waiting downstairs. Satisfied she was dressed and ready for battle, well, dinner at least, she headed for the door.

An evening with Jackson wasn't the worst thing on the planet, was it?

Six

Jackson felt it the moment Kristin arrived at the Caribbean-style soul food restaurant. The air seemed to shimmer just for a second, then settle in place. She'd always had that effect. That effortless way of attracting attention even though she was oblivious to it most of the time. He stood as the hostess brought Kristin over to the table.

She looked like she'd dressed to kill. He allowed himself to take in her inimitable sense of style as she walked toward the table.

"Thank you for coming," he said when she reached him. He helped her settle in her chair and sat opposite.

"Can I get you a drink while you look at the menu?" the hostess asked. "Your waiter will be along shortly to take your orders."

"Kristin, would you like a drink?" he asked.

"Do you think that's safe?" she teased with a mock-serious look on her face.

He'd always loved her ability to poke fun at herself when she'd done something silly or just plain wrong. It was good to see she hadn't lost her humor after what he'd done to her.

"I'm sure you can be trusted," he said with a slow smile.

"Then I'll have one of these." She pointed to a locally made chardonnay from the Columbia Valley on the wine list.

"We'll share a bottle," he said to the hostess as he passed the wine list to her.

"My, you are trusting, aren't you?" Kristin gibed as the hostess walked away. "Aren't you worried I'll make another scene?"

He sighed and looked at her across the table. "Look, I understand that seeing each other again last Friday was a shock, but didn't we agree to put that behind us and move forward?"

"You're right," she said succinctly. "I guess I'm just more embarrassed about my behavior than I'm prepared to admit."

"No need. Just two old friends, remember?"

"Yeah, right."

She picked up her menu and studied it carefully. She was obviously avoiding eye contact with him. He looked at her slender hands with their long fingers holding the menu. As feminine and delicate as they were, she still looked all business, with short, clear-polished nails.

"I'll have the gumbo," she said decisively after only a couple of minutes.

"You don't want to think about that? Change your mind a hundred times?"

She gave him a wry smile at the pointed reminder of what she used to be like when they were going out. It had been a running joke that he wouldn't order until she'd changed her mind at least three times.

"I'm quite certain, thank you. You may not have changed in the past eleven years, but I have."

He accepted the barb with a nod of his head. "Gumbo sounds good to me, too."

A wine waiter came over with their chardonnay and offered it to Jackson to taste.

"Perhaps Ms. Richmond should taste it as it is her choice," he said, gesturing to the young man.

Jack watched as Kristin went through the motions of tasting the wine.

"Yes, thank you, that will do nicely," she said with a smile.

They were silent as the waiter poured their glasses and left them. Kristin took another sip, then set her glass on the crisp white tablecloth.

"So, what did you want to talk about?" she asked, coming straight to the point.

"I realize you didn't want to discuss this in your office, but we need to clear the air about our past," he said firmly.

"There's nothing to clear. The past is over," she said.

"Maybe for you, but I feel I have unfinished business."

"You do? Why now?"

Okay, so she wasn't going to make this easy. He could accept that. She'd been the wounded party, after all.

"I owe you an explanation—" he started, but she interrupted.

"You owe me nothing."

There was something in the way she'd said that last word that implied he both owed her nothing and meant nothing to her. At least not anymore. Even though they'd both moved on, it still sent a shaft of pain through him to know he'd hurt her. Not for the first time, he wished he could turn back the clock and do everything differently. But he knew that was impossible.

"Humor me, okay?"

"Fine." She lifted her glass and took another sip of wine, this time holding on to the glass as she patiently waited for him to continue.

He'd rehearsed this a dozen times already and yet, when it came to saying the words, it was a whole lot harder than he'd expected. He took a deep breath and began.

"You remember how I would never talk about my family?"

"I accepted it wasn't a subject that you were happy to discuss. I figured you'd tell me when you were ready. Except you were never ready, were you?"

He sighed again. "No, I wasn't. I'm not sure I am

even now. It's not a subject I'm comfortable discussing, but this needs to be brought into the open. My family wasn't like yours."

"What, based on lies and deceit?" she said sarcastically.

She put her glass down again and fiddled with her napkin instead, alerting him to how nervous she was.

"Well, perhaps like you believed your family to be back then. My upbringing was very different from yours. Sure, we had plenty of money—that was never the problem."

"What was the problem?" she asked, swiftly catching on.

"My dad was our city mayor, and he thrived on the attention and responsibility that came with his position. Mom, too. You'd have thought she was First Lady, to be honest. But despite the public facade, my parents' marriage was dysfunctional. They were passionate about each other almost to the exclusion of everyone around, and they'd quarrel as passionately as they loved. Violently, too. Oh, I'd be paraded out at the appropriate times, and they'd say how proud they were of how well I did at school. But that was the family picture they presented when they had to. Behind closed doors it was a different story, especially if I didn't bring home excellent grades. My father wasn't averse to beating his expectations into me, or my mother."

"Oh, Jackson. I had no idea. I'm so sorry."

"Nothing for you to be sorry for. It was what it was. I still struggle knowing my mother never saw her role as a nurturing one or that my father thought he had the right to ignore me at will. As I got older, their focus on each other became even more intense. Their fights, also. Heading to college set me free of all that.

"I got the call that they'd both been killed in a car wreck on the morning of our graduation. You'd already gone to meet your parents. I didn't know what to do. I just grabbed my things and left. I had to get home. I had to see them. I had to talk to the police. They were saying Mom was driving, and they suspected she deliberately took the car over the edge of the road into a ravine. There were no skid marks on the road. Mom had left a note at the house for me. She said she'd had enough but because she couldn't bear a future without him, she'd decided to take both their lives.

"The investigation concluded murder-suicide. The local press had a field day."

Kristin looked at him across the table, raw compassion in her eyes. "Jackson, you must have felt so alone. I wish you had reached out to me. I would have been there for you."

"I know, but I didn't want you involved in the mess that was my family. Or the attention my parents' deaths garnered in the media. I remember you saying how much your family guarded its privacy, and how publicity-shy they were. Everyone I knew was being dragged into the mire my mother left behind. I couldn't tangle you up in that. It was simpler to excise myself from your life."

She shook her head. "I know I don't need to say it, but I am truly sorry for what you went through. And more so that you didn't feel like you could reach out to me. Even when the dust settled."

"But it never really settles, does it? The taint lies over your life." Jackson took a sip of his wine. "I've talked to counselors about this and learned to process how my mom's choice that day affected me. But the fact remains I walked out on you, on us, on our dreams for a future, and I never addressed that. I'm sorry, Kristin. I should have at least spoken to you, told you I was leaving."

"Yes, you should have, but you must have been in shock. It hurt when I realized you were gone. I felt as if my heart had been cut out, as if everything we'd had together was a lie. I went from loving you to hating you and back again so many times. I struggled with trust after that—I still do. Your choice to leave me so abruptly changed me."

He took every word she said and absorbed it like a bullet. He knew he'd hurt her, but he hadn't expected her hurt to have been so absolute or to have changed the open, happy and sunny woman he'd fallen in love with back in college, to one who was harder and less trusting. The sense of responsibility he bore for that was monumental. Somehow, he had to make it up to her.

"*Sorry* is such a pathetic word. I don't know what to say to you, Kristin. I can't undo time or rewrite the past, but I can promise you that I won't let you or your family down now. I understand you don't trust me, and you have good reason for that, but I will do my best as your family's attorney."

The waiter arrived with their orders, making further conversation awkward for the next minute or so. Once the waiter had gone, though, he leaned forward and took Kristin's hand from where it sat on the table surface.

"Can you believe me now, Kristin? Can you learn to trust that I won't abandon my duty to your family?"

She tugged her hand loose and looked at him across the table. "I don't know. I need some time to think about what you've told me. And I also need to see that you really do mean what you say. After all, you made promises to me before. While the circumstances of you leaving were anyone's worst nightmare, you never made a single attempt to contact me in the intervening time. Not even a text to acknowledge you were still alive. Can you imagine the different scenarios I went through in my mind when I couldn't get ahold of you?"

Regret was a fiercely painful thing to acknowledge. He'd been young and grief-stricken, more for what his family should have been than what it actually was, and he'd made choices that had created a bad and far-reaching result for Kristin. It didn't matter how much he'd grown or changed in the interim, he couldn't undo the harm he'd done her.

"I will do my utmost to prove to you that you can rely on me. I know it's little compensation but if you have any doubts about my ability as an attorney, talk to Hector. He will assure you that I'm more than competent. Of course, only time will tell if you can allow yourself to trust me. I don't expect that you will ever forgive me for what I did, and I'm fine with that. No matter the circumstances, we were a couple, and I owed you an explanation. I was wrong to do what I did, and I'm deeply sorry for having hurt you so badly."

She looked at him for a while, her cool gray eyes piercing as she sat silently. Did she believe him? Would she give him a chance to prove himself as an attorney, if not as a man, to be depended on?

"Fine," she said abruptly. "I accept your apology. Now, can we eat?"

Just like that? He doubted she was satisfied, but at least she didn't get up and walk away.

"Thank you, Kristin."

"For what?"

"For listening. For accepting what I said."

"Jackson, your truth is your truth. You have to live with that. We all make our own choices. If I've become more cautious about people, including you, then that's my choice, and it's not entirely a bad thing."

He held her gaze for a moment longer than he should and felt a shift deep inside. One that felt familiar and yet new and exciting at the same time. She'd always been a beautiful girl, but now Kristin was a very beautiful woman and he was no less affected by her now than the first time he'd seen her. He blinked, and the moment was lost. She lifted her spoon and tasted her gumbo, and he did the same, almost relieved to be released from the brief spell that had bound them.

Flavor exploded on his tongue, but there was something missing. Not in the food, which was sublime, but deep in his core. Knowing how his choices had irrevocably changed the woman in front of him gouged a gaping hole in him that he knew only time and dogged determination to always do the right thing by her would heal. Could he do the hard yards to get there? To help her to rediscover the woman she used to be before he changed her perspective on life so drastically?

He had to.

Seven

"So, have you had any further correspondence from the new claimant yet?" Kristin asked as they lingered over coffee after their meal.

She watched as Jackson dabbed at his mouth with his napkin and sat back in his chair. He still had that effortless grace about him in everything he did. It drove her crazy that he hadn't grown clumsy or lost his finesse, anything to make him less physically appealing. But then she only had to remind herself that looks were just skin-deep. The measure of a man came in how he treated others, no matter the circumstances.

"Nothing aside from a read receipt on the reply I sent to them. I expect I'll get more in the way of a reply tomorrow or possibly the day after. I doubt they'll provide me with the original documents I requested, but we do need to see copies and DNA info. I have pointed out that they are advised to appoint a legal representative. If they are prepared to do that, then we will take the next steps to prove the veracity of the claim. In the meantime, our IT people have researched the IP address of the sender. From what we can tell they're hosted somewhere in Tacoma, which ties into the mailing office address for their original contact. The police would be able to find out more but at this point we will continue our investigation per Nancy's request."

She pondered the situation for a moment before speaking. "You know, given what we've learned my father was capable of, it's entirely possible that their claim is correct. If that's true, what will that mean for our family?"

"You're the first person to ask me that. Everyone else has basically circled the wagons and metaphorically hunkered down. Okay, let's see, if the claim is genuine, it may mean potentially reducing your shareholdings in Richmond Developments and possibly, for your other siblings, in Richmond Construction, to release funds. Hector's notes show that each family has opted not to take shares in the West or East Coast equivalent that your father established, but if this person is indeed a potential beneficiary, they would likely want a piece of all the pies, so to speak."

"And what if there are more claims?" she asked, dreading the answer.

"Then your father's estate could continue to be tied up for years. His business succession plan was clear, though and his legal acknowledgement of Logan as his missing son preempted any potential issues there. While other as yet unknown children may be able to make a claim on his assets, the actual running of the companies remains in the named children's hands."

She groaned. "It's all such a darn mess, isn't it?"

"Don't worry for now. Worry achieves nothing. We have to work through the situation methodically and ensure that the claim is valid before it becomes an issue."

"You make it all sound so logical when for us it's very emotional."

"I can understand that, but honestly, my gut feeling is that this person is trying to capitalize on your family's aversion to risk and public exposure. I doubt there is any veracity to their assertions, and I would hazard a guess to say that's why they've requested a monetary sum versus shares in the companies."

She fought a smile. On legal matters he managed to sound so pompous. Quite a different man to the one she'd enjoyed debating with on social issues while they were in college. Sometimes she'd take the opposite side of an argument just so they could have a heated discussion, which would always end with them ripping off each other's clothes and making their point with their bodies rather than words. Just thinking about those times sent an uncomfortable rush of heat through her body and she shifted in her chair.

"Well," she said forcing her lips into a smile. "Let's hope you're right. Now, thank you for inviting me tonight. Perhaps we can split the bill and I'll be on my way."

"No, this is on me. Do you have your car here?"

"No."

"Then please, let me see you home."

"So you can report to my mother that I'm safe and sound?" she said archly.

He laughed, and she was caught for a moment by the expression on his face and the way his laughter lightened everything about his features. It reminded her so much of the man she'd fallen in love with so long ago. Sure, the crinkles at the corners of his eyes were deeper and his forehead a little more careworn, but essentially he was still the same person. Again, she felt that physical surge of interest swell through her body. Again, she tamped it down. Physical attraction was all well and good, but it only led to heartbreak, no matter how many apologies were issued later.

"Something like that," he concurred.

Jackson gestured for the check and dealt with it promptly, then rose from his seat and helped Kristin from her chair. She was usually not a fan of this kind of old-fashioned courtesy, but for some reason that she didn't want to go into any deeper, it felt right with him.

"Did you bring a coat?" he asked as they approached the door together.

She gestured to the fine black woolen coat hanging near the door to the restaurant and he helped her put it on. His fingers brushed her neck for the briefest second as he straightened her collar. She caught her gasp behind firmly closed lips before it could alert him to her reaction. Even so, the sensation of his touch left its brand on her skin. Left her craving more. This was stupid, she told herself. She shouldn't be feeling like this over a man she hadn't seen in eleven years. A man who'd stomped all over her heart along with their plans for their future. A man whom she now couldn't seem to get out of her thoughts.

"Are you parked far away?" she asked, taking a step away from him.

"Just around the corner."

They walked outside in the cool, damp evening air. Thankfully, there was no rain tonight, and they walked side by side to the car. When they neared the vehicle, the lights flashed discreetly as the car unlocked, and Jackson held the passenger door open for her. She settled herself and put on her seat belt, and as he sat next to her she couldn't help but breathe in his scent. He wore a crisp cologne, but beneath it was a layer that was essentially him. A scent she knew on the most primal level that a woman could know a man.

She was glad her apartment was nearby, because being alone with him like this was a lot harder than she'd ever imagined. Now that the fierce anger of seeing him again had burned off and he'd told her about his past, she couldn't quite summon the barriers that her fury had provided. She resolved that from now on, she'd avoid seeing him on her own. After all, they had no reason to be together now that they'd cleared the air. In future, all dealings would be done by video, phone or in a group with her family to bolster her defenses. The last thing Kristin needed was to fall for him all over again.

At her apartment building, she was quick to let herself out of the car. She leaned down to say good-night and thank-you, before closing the door and walking smartly toward the main doors of the complex. Behind her she heard the car idling as Jackson waited for her to go inside. She fought the urge to turn and wave. That was the action of someone who gave a damn, and, she told herself, she didn't.

Knowing why he'd left the way he did didn't absolve him entirely. Oh, yes, she was compassionate enough to understand his reaction to the horrific news he'd received. But to cease all contact? She didn't know if she'd ever accept that or trust him fully again. And as for his reliability as their attorney, while he appeared to be doing all the right things, it remained to be proven that he was the best man for the job.

Kristin entered her building and with a nod to the night guard stationed at the desk, went to the elevators. Upstairs in her apartment, she walked to the window that overlooked the street. His car was gone and she felt an odd pang of loss seeing he was no longer there.

"Don't be stupid," she warned herself out loud. "You've been down that road. You're not going there again."

It was later that week that she agreed to meet her mom for lunch near Pike Place Market. Nancy had asked for her help with some of the wedding planning, and Kristin couldn't say no, no matter how heavy her workload. Nancy was already seated at a window table overlooking the water, when Kristin arrived.

"I ordered for you. I know you're pressed for time and you're just going to get clam chowder and sourdough bread anyway," Nancy said on a laugh.

Kristin examined her mom. She hadn't seen her look so happy or so carefree since Douglas Richmond died. It did her heart good to see her like that.

"You're looking great, Mom. And thanks for ordering. Is it sad that I'm so predictable?"

"Not at all. There's safety in predictability. While you might have been more adventurous as a child, since you came home from college you've been careful and considered in your choices."

And there was yet another reminder about how much Jackson Jones had changed her outlook on life. On everything, to be honest.

"I'm boring, aren't I? Just say it," Kristin said with a laugh.

"Careful, I'd say. But not afraid to say what you

think, which is what I've always loved about you. Among other things, of course." Nancy reached across the table and patted Kristin on the hand. "Tell me, darling. Was it Jackson Jones who broke your spirit?"

Kristin felt the air in her lungs leave in a giant whoosh, leaving her trapped in a vacuum where sound and logic temporarily ceased to exist. How on earth had her mother deduced that so quickly? She forced herself to draw in a breath, then another, and slowly the noise of the patrons around them, the music in the speakers, and the sounds of waiters moving about began to filter back in.

"What makes you ask that, Mom?" she asked, opting for deflection versus actually answering the question.

Her mother nodded. "Okay, I get the hint. Your response is all the answer I need. I always suspected that there was a man behind the change in you when you came home from college. I know your father paid your full tuition on condition that you didn't date while you were studying, and I always wondered why. I guess we all know now, don't we? Douglas probably didn't want to take the risk you'd meet up with one of your half siblings. So, back to Jackson—shall we fire him?"

Kristin blinked hard, then stared at her mother in shock. "You'd do that?"

"He hurt my baby girl. Is he the kind of man we want looking after us? You tell me."

"Mom, it was a long time ago, and we were very

young and very different people then. If he steps out of line, then yes, we'll show him the door, but Hector trusts him and you trust Hector, right?" Her mom nodded. "Let's leave things as they are, okay?"

"One day, you'll tell me what happened."

"It's water under the bridge now."

"If you say so. Oh, look, here's our lunch."

They ate their meals and conversation turned toward the wedding, which Nancy and Hector wanted to celebrate on New Year's Eve.

"It seemed appropriate to us that we see the New Year in as husband and wife. A symbol of starting our new life together. Obviously, we'd like to keep the guest list small and intimate. Invite just family and a few close friends. We'll have it at home. And I'd like to ask you to do a favor for me."

"Anything, Mom."

"Would you be my maid of honor?"

"I'd be delighted. Does that mean I get to catch your bouquet?" Kristin smiled.

"Only if you want to," Nancy said with a wink. "Of course, you'll be partnered with Hector's best man. I hope that won't cause any issues."

Kristin thought she'd met all of Hector's contemporaries at some stage over the years. Their families had been good friends even when his wife was still alive. She'd died about fifteen years ago. How bad could it be to be partnered with someone his age? At least they'd hopefully be able to do a decent turn on the dance floor when the time came.

"Issues?"

"With Jackson."

"*He's* going to be Hector's best man?"

"Not if you don't want him to be. Hector and I discussed this, especially in light of your response to meeting him last week. Our wedding is going to be a wonderful celebration of the gift of our love but I don't want it to be a trial for you. Hector agrees with me."

"Mom, seriously, don't worry. Hector must have whomever he wants as his attendant at the wedding. We're all mature enough and sensible enough to be civil with one another."

At her mother's arched brow, Kristin felt a heated flush of embarrassment stain her cheeks.

"Okay, so I wasn't acting mature or sensible last Friday, but Jackson and I have spoken on at least two separate occasions now and we've managed to be extremely adult about everything. Everything will be fine."

Even though she spoke with confidence, Kristin couldn't help but cross the fingers of one hand in her lap. Her mom beamed.

"Thank you, darling. You mean the world to me, and I hate seeing you unhappy. This past year has been tough on all of us, but you most of all, I think. I look forward to seeing that beautiful smile of yours more often."

Kristin made a mental note to try harder for her mom and decided that a change of subject was in order.

"Have you decided what you're going to wear? Will the wedding be during the day, or evening?"

"Evening, so we can party the night away. As to a dress, I thought the one I wore to the last Richmond Foundation dinner would be suitable. I've only worn it once."

"Oh no, you can't wear something you already own!" Kristin protested.

"Why not? It's something old, like me," Nancy said with a self-deprecating laugh.

"Because it's your *wedding*. I know you and Dad had a whirlwind courtship and chose a registry office wedding, so I think you deserve to have all the trimmings this time around. And I'd like it to be my gift to you. Please, don't argue with me on this. Let's make a date to go shopping on the weekend. I'm sure we'll find something that's perfect for you."

Her mom's eyes filled with tears of joy. "If it means so much to you, then, yes, I accept."

Kristin smiled at her mom and felt like she'd done something right for the first time in a long time. The wedding would be everything her mom's heart desired, because she deserved the very best. Not for one moment had she faltered in her dignity or her love for her family. Not through the grief of Logan's kidnapping, or the shock of having him return more than thirty years later. Nor when she was hit by the sudden death of her husband followed by the awful revelation about his second wife and kids.

Nancy Richmond was style and class and a mother's love all wrapped into one incredible package. Kristin needed to take a leaf from her mother's book and learn to cope the way she did. Maybe then she'd feel like she had some kind of control over her life again.

Back in the office, Kristin made a decision. It was past time she stopped shouldering all the responsibility of her department on her own. There were a couple of potential candidates in the finance team who could, and likely deserved to, take on the role left vacant by Isaac's departure. People she knew and trusted to do the job right. It would surely be easier to fill one of their roles, either internally or by taking on a college graduate, than to allow a rank outsider into the company into a position of relative power. She made a call to the new head of HR and set out her parameters. She listed the three staff members in her department she thought might be suitable for the promotion and requested they be contacted regarding their interest in the role. By the time she got off the phone she felt like ceremoniously dusting off her hands and congratulating herself on a job well done. There, she was making changes and delegating control.

Her thoughts turned to her mom's upcoming wedding, and she quickly searched suitable retail outlets that stocked the kind of thing her mom might like to wear for the wedding, and that would carry something she could buy for her role as maid of honor, too. She made a list and added them to the calendar in her phone, together with GPS coordinates so they could make the most of their day.

The wedding would be lovely, and her mom would look beautiful. She wondered just how much time she and Jackson would have to spend together at the event. Her mom was big on observing old-style etiquette whenever she could and often said that people were sadly losing sight of the common courtesies and expectations of the past. They'd probably be expected to have at least one dance together. How would that feel, being held in his arms again? She pushed the thought away as quickly as it had surfaced, but not before she felt a definite kick of interest unfurl from deep inside.

She tried to tamp down the sensation but it stubbornly wouldn't budge, so she defaulted to what had worked for her in the past. Anger. She got good and mad at Jackson Jones all over again. Heck, at all the men who'd let her down over the years, Isaac and her father included. But while Isaac's betrayal had been a vicious blow, her father's deception had been the cruelest. He'd been her rock. The measure by which any guy she went out with was compared to. And he'd turned out to be a fake. Well, she conceded, not entirely a fake because he had, apparently, loved both his wives and both his families very much. But he had deceived all of them with his duplicity and that had, directly or indirectly, brought Jackson back into her sphere.

Kristin got up from her desk and went to the window. It had started to rain. The dreary weather was a perfect representation of how she felt right now. She'd thought she had everything so right in her life. That she was achieving both her work and relationship goals. On the work front, they were now clawing to hold their place in the construction market, their strength having been undermined by the scandal of her father's double life and the subsequent espionage attempt by Warren Everard, and her private life had imploded. All her hopes for her future washing away like the rain skating down the sheet glass windows facing her.

She drew in a long, deep breath and let it go again. It wasn't like her to dwell on the past. But when the past came up to you and whacked you on the side of your head, you had to find a new way of coping. She would do that, because she was a survivor, she told herself sternly. She adapted. She thrived. She carried on. And she would do exactly that.

Eight

Jackson checked his email from home before the short commute into the office. He found it helped to be totally prepared; during his drive in, he could let his subconscious mull on any issues that had arisen and be able to act on them by the time he got to his desk. It was ten days since his dinner with Kristin and there'd been no further correspondence on the Richmond estate claim, so he wasn't surprised to see a new email in his inbox from the claimant. It had several attachments.

He opened the email and scanned its contents quickly. The claimant reissued their demand for money with a repeat of the January 7 deadline for payment. Now, though, they added a threat to start leaking news about their claim and their mother's affair with Douglas Richmond to the media if they didn't receive at least half the payment by December 31. A bank account number was included in the email. He grunted. This really didn't sit well with him. The matter needed to be put into the hands of the police, whose resources to trace who was behind the claim were far more extensive than his. But he had to be guided by the family's wishes.

Jackson clicked on the attachments to view what were obviously scanned photographs of who he presumed to be Douglas Richmond, or someone who looked very much like him, and a much younger woman with blond hair and a pretty smile. In themselves, the photos were hardly incriminating, until you looked at the placement of Douglas's hand on the woman next to him. His arm was around the woman's back, but his hand was higher than her waist, almost under her breast, as if he were sneakily caressing her breast with his thumb. It potentially suggested an intimacy between them that might not have been immediately obvious to others around them.

If this photo had not been doctored in any way and indeed was that of a boss with a staff member, there were obvious questions to be asked. First, was the woman in the photo a willing participant in what was a very intimate touch, or was this a case of sexual harassment? Was that the reason behind the payment this person claimed Douglas had made to their mother? Jackson made some notes on his phone to follow up with the HR department at Richmond Developments on staff records from the time the claimant said their mother worked for the company. If he could establish her identity, it would also help track down the claimant.

By the time he arrived in the office, he had a to-do list as long as his forearm on the Richmond matter, which didn't bode too well for any other client activity today. Still, Hector had built a great team in the practice and a lot of the work could be allocated to junior lawyers or interns, so that was exactly what Jackson would do where he could. He was relieved that his arrival at the firm had been well received. It meant he got the support he needed, when he needed it and, right now, it was important to him to get this matter with the Richmond family sorted out as quickly and calmly as possible. He owed it to them and to his friendship with Hector to get it 100 percent right all the way. And even though they'd cleared the air between them, he still had something to prove to Kristin, too.

He knew only too well how hard it was to earn trust from another person and how easy it was to lose it. He'd had to work darn hard to get Annie to look at him as anything other than a junior partner in the law firm where they practiced. She'd mentored him, encouraged him, coached him and done all the things that helped to make him a fine attorney. But she'd been dead set against allowing him to woo her.

It had taken a couple of years, but eventually he'd worn down her resistance and shown her that he was steadfast in his feelings for her and that the disparity in their ages meant nothing to him. It was only then that he'd learned about how she'd had a workplace relationship with an older man when she first passed the bar, and how she was unceremoniously dumped and fired when she'd gotten pregnant. Her trust had been shattered, and to protect herself and her special needs son she'd become careful about whom she allowed into her life and her heart.

Becoming a stepdad to a person only a few years his junior had brought its challenges, even if Ben had the mental age of a six-year-old. But his relationship with Annie's son had grown to such a point that Ben looked forward to spending time with him and he with Ben, also. In fact, they had a special evening planned this week. Pizza and a movie marathon. Ben had mostly settled well into the residential care facility here in Seattle, but he looked forward to his visits with Jack.

Jackson settled at his desk and was halfway into composing an email to a forensic image analyst he worked with to see if the claimant's photos had been altered—when the phone on his desk buzzed.

"Yes?" he answered, his tone short.

"Sorry, Mr. Jones. I know you asked not to be disturbed but it's Mr. Ramirez on the phone, and it sounds urgent."

"Thank you, put him through." Jackson waited a couple of seconds until Hector came on the line. "Hector, how are you, my friend?"

"Not so good, I'm afraid."

The man sounded terrible, his voice shaky and weak.

"Do you need my help?" Jackson asked.

"No, no. It looks like Nancy and I have a bad dose of stomach flu. We've seen the doctor, but we've been warned to remain isolated from other people for a few more days."

"Sorry to hear that, Hector. Do you need anything at the house? Is Martha okay?" Jackson's mind raced through the possibilities of what he could do to help out his friend if their housekeeper was also ill.

"No, she's fine. She's preparing meals for us and sanitizing everything we touch or use. The woman has been an incredible help. We'll be okay. In fact we're pretty much on the mend now, but I desperately need you to do a favor for us."

"Name it."

"We were supposed to be attending a gala for the Richmond Foundation on Thursday evening. We won't be clear to socialize by then and I was hoping you could take my place. You don't have to make any speeches or anything like that. Just smile and shake a few hands, thank the donors when they're introduced to you by the organizers, that sort of thing."

Jackson knew what was expected of him. He'd attended many such events with Annie, who'd been the patron of a charity that worked to benefit children, like Ben, who'd been brain-damaged at birth.

"Hector, I have another appointment for that evening. Let me check with them, and I'll get back to you as soon as I can."

They ended the call, and Jackson gave a sigh of frustration. It was always the way, wasn't it? He had booked that evening to spend with Ben, and now this had come up. He couldn't let Hector down, though, and it was part of his role as the family's attorney to attend events like this. Hector had initially told him he was off the hook for this one because he and Nancy had been looking forward to it. Jack only hoped that changing the date on his stepson on short notice wouldn't inconvenience or upset him.

Another phone call later, Jackson called Hector. "I'm good to go."

"Excellent, thank you. Nancy and I do appreciate this."

"Has Nancy asked someone else to go in her stead?"

There was a slight hesitation on the other end before Hector answered. "Yes, she has asked Kristin to attend."

"Does Kristin know I would be escorting her?"

Again there was a small pause, as if he were conferring with Nancy, before Hector answered. "Not yet, but that won't be a problem. Nancy tells me that you two have sorted out your differences, yes?"

"Yes," Jackson said, although he didn't for one minute believe that Kristin had forgiven him for what he'd done to her, nor likely ever would.

"Then that's all settled. We'll courier the event invitations to you and the car has already been booked. It'll collect you first, then Kristin, and take you to the venue."

For just a minute, Jackson wondered if he was being manipulated by his older friend who suddenly sounded a lot less shaky and weak than he had in the earlier call. But then he shrugged that off. Hector wasn't into sneaky machinations. In fact, he was one of the most open and up-front people that Jackson had ever had the pleasure to know. But Hector was a romantic at heart, and if he'd thought he could engineer a reunion of long-lost lovers, he probably would have a stab at it. Jackson shook his head. No, he was being ridiculous. Hector was way too wrapped up in his own romance to be trying to engineer someone else's. It would only be natural for Jackson and Kristin to attend in Hector and Nancy's stead. He was overthinking things, the way he always did.

"Now that's settled, you two hurry up and get well again, okay?"

"We will. By the way, what's the latest on the Richmond family case?"

Jackson got Hector up to speed with the email and its contents that he'd received that morning and told Hector his plans for the forensic image analyst.

"Sounds like a good idea," the older man said approvingly. "What's your gut feeling on the case?"

"I don't like it. And I'm starting to really not like Douglas Richmond. I know you two were friends, but if this guy treated his female staff like the guy in this photo is doing, he wasn't a very nice man at all. That said, I still don't think the claim is genuine. My gut feeling, since you asked, is that someone who might be in contact with the family in some peripheral way is trying to cash in on their media and publicity shyness and is hoping for some kind of payout."

"I agree," Hector said on a sigh. "But until we

know for certain, we have to tread carefully. As to what Douglas was really like—I don't believe that anyone but Douglas knew who the real Douglas Richmond was. He was very good at making you see exactly what he wanted you to see."

"He must have been a very clever man."

"It was a huge part of his charm. Like the rest of his family, he had me thoroughly duped. I've been wondering who my best friend was, after all. Yes, I believe he was capable of having had other affairs. But his focus on his children and their achievements was such that I believe he would have wanted to have a major influence in the life of any other child of his. Like you, I smell a rat with this one. Keep up the good work."

They ended the call and Jackson focused on the rest of his day, which included emailing a summary of the latest contact from their anonymous claimant, together with the photo of Douglas and the mystery woman, to the Richmond family. Kristin was the first to acknowledge receipt of his email and replied with one of her own.

I hear we are attending Mom's gala together. It's black tie. I hope you have the right attire. :)

He smiled at the not-so-subtle reminder and formulated his response.

Rest assured, I will be at your apartment building at the appropriate time and dressed in the appropriate garb.

She replied immediately.

Good to know. BTW, did this potential love child of Dad's include a photo of themselves or even answer any of your questions from your original reply to them?

Jackson typed a negative response and saw Kristin's reply landing in his inbox.

Figures.

It's early days. We will get to the bottom of this.

He waited a couple of minutes for her to reply again but she'd obviously been distracted by something else, so he returned his attention to the work in front of him.

Thursday night rolled around all too quickly. He'd hoped to get a response from the forensics image analyst, but apparently there was a backlog and no inducement could push their request to the head of the line.

The tuxedo he wore was bespoke, and he knew he looked sharp tonight. He left his Eastlake floating home and walked to the pickup area to meet the vehicle that was collecting him tonight. The first time he'd ever visited Seattle with Annie, to visit her parents, he was fascinated by the homes literally built on the water at the edge of Lake Union so when he knew he was moving here, he didn't bother looking for a home anywhere else. Sure, parking was problematic, but it was worth it for the lakeside living.

The trip to Kristin's apartment building passed quickly, and through the glass of the lobby, he spied her the moment she exited the elevator and began to walk to the main doors.

He was glad of the opportunity to watch her walking as if she owned the world and looking as if she did, too. She reminded him of one of those glamorous silver screen stars of yesteryears as she stepped out. Her gown was gold and floor-length, and moved along with her every step as if it was a living being. Her sleeves were made of some gossamer-fine sheer fabric that was full over her arms but caught in delicate diamanté-studded cuffs at her wrists. The same shimmer of glitter hung from her ears, accentuating the long line of her neck exposed by her updo. The neckline of her dress was a deep V, giving him a tantalizing glimpse of the delicate roundness of her breasts. She'd always been a beautiful woman, but tonight, with her cheekbones highlighted by careful contouring and her eyes made up in smoky shades of gray, she was absolutely captivating.

Again she wore the striking red lipstick that she'd worn the other night to dinner, and despite his better intentions, he imagined what it would be like to kiss that luscious color off her lips. A shaft of guilt speared through him. He shouldn't be thinking about Kristin this way. It was as if, by craving her, he was being unfaithful to Annie's memory, and that scored a line through his heart like nothing else had done since the day she died.

Reminding himself he was here as Kristin's escort, and nothing else, Jackson rose from the car and held the door open for her as she approached. She swept him with a look that went from the top of his head to the shine on his shoes then up again.

"You'll do," she said succinctly, before sliding onto the rear passenger seat of the car.

"You scrub up pretty well, yourself," he commented in return before he closed the door and walked around to the other side and got in. With both of them in the vehicle, the driver slid up the privacy glass between the front and rear compartments, sealing them in a private cocoon.

"In fact, you look beautiful tonight," he said.

"Maybe if everyone else agrees with you they'll forgive me for being nervous about giving Mom's speech," she said with a slight tremor in her voice.

She was nervous? He was incredulous that this insanely confident-looking creature beside him could ever feel such a thing. But then he remembered how much she'd hated presenting group assignments to their class and how sometimes she'd be sick before painting on a brave face and giving yet another winning presentation.

"Have you thrown up yet?" he asked.

"Not yet, but that doesn't mean it isn't going to happen." She firmed her lips into a straight line and looked across at him. "I can't believe you still remember that about me."

"I remember a great deal about you, Kristin," he said with painful honesty.

She snorted in disbelief and turned her head to look out the window. "I always thought that once I was out of sight I was out of mind."

"I often wished it could have been that easy," he answered softly.

She was silent for a few moments, then looked across at him again. "What made you choose law?"

"I liked the idea of helping people and it turned out that I was good at it."

"So modest of you," she teased lightly.

He shrugged. "I was pretty darn successful in litigation in California."

"So, why Seattle, now? And why the change in legal specialization?"

"It was time for a change."

It was past time. The finesse of what he'd done in the litigation field had begun to tarnish for him around the time Annie had first taken ill. His partners had been supportive when he'd said he was taking a year off to care for her, but when she'd passed away so soon after her diagnosis and they'd pressured him to come back, he realized he hadn't been enjoying his work for a long time. He'd given up his partnership and taken time off to heal from his loss. It hadn't been easy.

To keep his mind sharp, he'd done pro bono work at community advice centers near his home and he'd found the taste of general law intriguing. So, when Hector had called him to discuss Annie's wish that

Ben be relocated to Seattle to be nearer his grandparents and offered him the opportunity to buy the practice and take on the senior partner role at Ramirez Law, the timing was perfect. It had given him the fresh start he desperately needed.

"Why'd you want a change?" she asked.

"I guess it's what you seek when you're no longer satisfied with where you are. Don't get me wrong, my litigation work was fulfilling but I'd lost my joy in it. It's always been my goal to deliver my very best to my clients and if I'm not passionate about what I'm doing, how can I be certain I'm giving my best?"

"We always had that in common, didn't we?"

"Doing our best? Yeah."

She fell silent and stared out the window again, her hand clenching around the glittery evening bag she held in her lap. As they drew up in the line of cars waiting to drop off their passengers at the venue, he reached across and patted her hand.

"You're going to be fine. You know that. You always did great."

"Thanks for the vote of confidence."

Their vehicle drew up at the head of the line, and they joined the throng on the carpet runner leading up the stairs to the main entrance. There was a strong media presence; no doubt that would augur well for the Richmond Foundation and the work they were doing. He took Kristin's hand and tucked it through his arm. Her hand trembled as it rested on his forearm.

"Just smile and wave, boys. Smile and wave," he murmured in her ear.

She laughed. "I can't believe you're still quoting from a kids' movie."

"Hey, if it gets us through this line, let's just do it."

She gave a short laugh but with her free hand did as he'd suggested. They avoided most of the questions being flung toward them until they were held up just a few feet from the front door. A reporter with a press pass identifying her as being from a local newspaper's gossip column leaned over the velvet ropes and directed a question at Kristin.

"Ms. Richmond, your family has had a tumultuous year, to say the least. Should we be prepared for more surprises in the future?"

He heard Kristin's sharply indrawn breath and felt her stiffen. In that moment, Jackson knew he'd do whatever it took to protect her from the prying enquiry.

"Ignore her," he muttered under his breath. "Don't give her any bait to work with." Then he turned to the journalist and said, "Ms. Richmond is happy to discuss the work of the Richmond Foundation with you inside once this evening's formalities are concluded and that is all."

"But I don't have a ticket," the reporter replied.

"Then I guess you'll need to phone Ms. Richmond's office for an appointment, won't you?"

"And you are?" the woman persisted.

"No one you need worry about," he responded

crisply and escorted Kristin through the main doors and into the foyer of the building.

"Thank you," Kristin said as they each accepted a glass of champagne from a circulating waiter. "Do you think they've had a tip-off about what's going on?"

He pressed his lips in a firm line and considered what had happened.

"No, I don't. The timing of the question was unfortunate. I don't believe the question was related to our claimant because the premature release of information would eliminate their negotiating power."

"Are you sure about that?"

He took a sip of his champagne and let it linger in his mouth a moment before swallowing and answering her question. "No, I'm not sure, but you can be certain I'll be looking into it tomorrow. But don't let that woman detract from tonight and what the foundation is achieving. Hector would tan my hide if I let that happen."

His response had the desired effect and wiped the look of worry off Kristin's face, replacing it with a small smile.

"Now that I would pay to see," she said.

"Look, there's Keaton and Tami. Shall we go over?" he said, distracting her once more.

She agreed and as they joined her brother and—judging by the large winking diamond on Tami's finger—soon-to-be sister-in-law, he mentally examined the fierce and powerful urge he'd had to protect Kristin, as the journalist had spoken. His emotions had been sharp and unexpected and continued to linger uncomfortably even after the doors to the dining room were opened and they were ushered to their seats. It was only after Kristin had successfully delivered her mom's speech that he realized why that had happened.

He still had feelings for Kristin Richmond. Feelings that brought back vivid memories of just how good they'd been together before he'd turned his back and gone on to make a new life. Feelings that, no matter how intense he knew they could be, he could not and would not act upon. The last time he and Kristin had been a couple, it had all but consumed him. Leaving her had been incredibly hard, but he'd had to do it because he didn't want her dragged into the mess that was his life after his parent's death. And now, his commitment to Annie's memory and his promise to look out for Ben were his priority. There was no room in his life for her as well. His feelings had to be put aside.

Nine

Kristin toasted with Tami as the evening progressed past the formalities and into the more social part of the function. She was hugely relieved the speech had gone well and she felt a whole lot better about it now it was over. Tami worked side by side with the Richmond Foundation and another charity that was dear to her heart, Our People, Our Homes. Tonight's fundraiser was designed to draw attention to the joint activities of the two organizations and to seek major sponsorship for affordable housing for struggling, low-income families. And the massive turnout for the event showed her mom's influence with the financial movers and shakers of the city.

She knew her mom and Tami worked well together. Kristin was so glad her brother Keaton had found love with Tami. While their personalities seemed different, they genuinely complemented each other. Keaton could be quite intense at times and Tami was the antithesis of that. It wasn't that she couldn't be serious when she needed to be, but more that she had a lightness of spirit that rubbed off on everyone around her.

"Your mom would have been proud of you tonight," Tami said with a huge grin and clinked her glass with Kristin's. "You did a great job."

"Thank you, and so did you. Seeing you up there, speaking so effortlessly, made me more aware than ever why we're doing this. It definitely helps to keep the end goal in mind when you have to make a speech, doesn't it? Helps you shed your nerves."

"If I hadn't seen you avoid eating your appetizer, I would never have known you were nervous," Tami said with a small laugh.

"Well, I'm not avoiding my plate when the main course is served, you can be sure of that," Kristin said emphatically.

She was starving now that the business side of things was behind her. The murmur of voices around them swelled as wine flowed and the servers began to bring out the main course plates. Being at a head table, they were among the first to be served, for which she was grateful. The servers were doing alternate drops of two different styles of meal for those who didn't have specific dietary requirements. When Kristin's plate was put in front of her, disappointment made her wrinkle her nose. It wasn't that she didn't like fricassee de pollo, it was that she preferred the rack of lamb in red wine jus. Just as she was about to pick up her fork, Jackson, who was seated beside her, lifted her plate and replaced it with his.

"You don't need to do that," she said.

"I know, but I also know that lamb is one of your favorites. You'd prefer it, right?"

"I do, thank you."

She decided that acceptance was far better than arguing the point, especially when there were a lot of eyes on her this evening. But it surprised her that he'd remembered something as small as whether she preferred lamb over chicken. And it made her wonder, what else did he remember? She gave herself a mental shake. No, she really didn't want to go down that path again.

The meal was delicious. Between the main course and dessert and coffee they watched a presentation by the executive director of Our People, Our Homes showing their achievements to date and the concept drawings for future plans. Kristin felt a huge swell of pride that their company and their foundation had a big hand in the success of the new venture. While her side of the business was finance, the presentation gave her a far better understanding of where the dollar amounts went and the good they did in the community.

By the time dessert was served, she was feeling mellow. Again, the plates were alternate drops, and she looked from the white chocolate cheesecake with mandarin drizzle on her plate to Jackson's chocolate mousse with Irish cream liqueur dressing with interest.

"Don't even think about it," he warned with a low growl.

She laughed. "You remember when we used to share dessert?"

"This is not that time," he said firmly and lifted his spoon to sample his mousse. He groaned in enjoyment.

"Don't be mean," she teased.

"Fine," he said on a long-suffering sigh. "Take half, but fair's fair, you give half of yours to me."

"Sounds like a plan," Kristin agreed and carefully excised half of her dessert and slid it onto his plate and waited patiently while he did the same with his.

Across the table, Keaton was watching them with interest. "Anyone looking at you two would think you'd been together for ages. Quite a change, little sis, from how you treated Jackson only a short while ago."

"Thank you for bringing that up, Keaton. I'm sure Mom brought you up to never remind a lady of her poor behavior." Kristin glared across the table at her brother.

"She did, but you're not a lady, you're my sister—oof! What was that for?" he finished with a hurt look at his fiancée.

Kristin smiled smugly at him, fully aware that Tami had kicked him soundly under the table. Tami merely planted a swift kiss on Keaton's cheek and smiled conspiratorially at Kristin.

"We women need to stick together," she said.

This evening was really turning out to be a surprise, Kristin thought as they turned their attention to the desserts. First of all, Jackson's expert handling of the reporter outside and then her speech going well. Then his indulging her over her food preferences, and now Tami's support against her brother's teasing. All in all, she had to admit she was actually starting to enjoy herself. An interesting concept, she thought, when the past year had been little more than putting out metaphorical fires at work and then struggling through the end of yet another relationship. Maybe things really were taking a turn for the better. And maybe, just maybe, Jackson working for the family would turn out okay despite all her earlier misgivings.

After their dishes were cleared, several tables were moved to make room for a large dance floor. By the time the band began to play, Kristin was feeling tired and ready to head home, but to her surprise, Jackson came toward her and held out a hand.

"I believe this is our dance," he said. "Hector informed me this afternoon that he and Nancy would have led the dancing tonight, so I guess that means it's now up to us."

"Really? Mom never said." Kristin took a quick look around the room and realized that no one else had yet taken to the floor. "I guess we'd better start the ball rolling, literally."

She accepted his hand. For a moment she lost herself in the sensation of his warm skin and the firm but gentle strength of his fingers as he drew her toward him. His arm curved around her, the palm settling at the small of her back, while the other hand held hers. They stepped out into the slow dance currently being played. He always had been a good mover, she thought wistfully as they expertly did their first turn around the dance floor and people began to join them. Whether it was sport, dancing or— No, she wouldn't go there. It was hard enough to keep any kind of control on her body when he was so very close to her; she didn't want to make things worse by remembering how he moved when he made love. And there it was, she had to go there. She groaned inwardly.

"Problem? Did I step on your toe?" he asked, a look of concern on his face.

"No, not at all," she said swiftly. "But do we need to do this for long?"

"Let's sit out the next one, okay?"

"Sure. And then maybe we can slip away? I don't know about you, but I put in a full day at the office today before getting ready for tonight. And tomorrow—"

"No problem. To be honest, I'm ready to head off, too."

Was he? He didn't look it, but then again, she'd noticed that he was very good at hiding what he was thinking or feeling. Probably a good trait in a lawyer when dealing with difficult clients or situations, but it made it hard for her to read him and she'd always considered herself to be a fairly decent judge of people. With the rank exception of Isaac, of course.

She looked into Jackson's blue eyes to see if she could tell if he was lying, but they remained unfathomable. There had been a time she'd always known what he was thinking, but not now. They were both very different people to who they'd been in college. She reminded herself she shouldn't care what he was thinking. After all, unless he was involved in the direct execution of his duty to her family, it was none of her business.

The band swung into an up-tempo piece and more people came onto the dance floor.

"I think that's our cue to leave, don't you?" Jackson said, bending his head slightly to murmur in her ear.

She tried to ignore the shiver of awareness that crept through her at his nearness and at the intimacy of his breath on her skin and took a step away from him.

"Yes, let's say our goodbyes to Tami and Keaton and we can be on our way."

At the table, Tami and Keaton looked as if they, too, were preparing to head home.

"Escaping, too?" Keaton asked with a grin.

"We've done our duty," Kristin said.

"Kristin, could you come with me to the ladies' room for a minute?" Tami asked.

Kristin looked at her in surprise. They were well past the age where they needed company to head to the bathroom, but one look at the expression on Tami's face made her agree and follow her to the bathrooms. The moment they were there, Tami swung and faced Kristin.

"Did you see it?" she asked.

"See what?"

She looked around the bathroom. It was empty except for the two of them.

"The tan line on his hand."

"The tan line on whose hand?" Kristin asked.

"Jackson's. I'd never noticed it before but there's a tan line on his finger."

"So the man wore a ring in the sun. It's not a crime, is it?"

"His *ring* finger."

Realization dawned slowly. "You think he's married?"

"Or very recently divorced. There's something between the two of you, isn't there?"

"There might have been once, long ago," Kristin admitted, still shocked at the thought of Jackson either being, or having been, married. She didn't know why it bothered her so much. After all, eleven years was a long time in which to have moved on. It wasn't like she still had any kind of claim on him. "But there's nothing now but a professional relationship."

"You say that but I've seen the way he looks at you and the way you two moved together on the dance floor. You were like a single unit. Totally in tune with each other."

"He's a good dancer," Kristin shrugged. "And that's all. Look, while we're here, I'm going to use the facilities."

She ducked into a stall and closed the door and wished it were as easy to close the door on the past. She had to admit it, to herself if no one else. It hurt to think of him with another woman. Logic dictated that it was bound to happen—even she'd had other relationships. But none that had truly captured her heart the way he had.

She exited the stall, determined not to let it bother her, and washed her hands before she and Tami returned to the men.

"So, are you going to ask him about it?" Tami asked.

"Why?"

Tami rolled her eyes. "To see if the coast is clear."

Kristin decided to play deliberately obtuse. "Coast?"

"Now I know you're avoiding the issue," Tami said with a quirk of her lips. "You're interested, aren't you? Why don't you ask him about his wife?"

"I'm avoiding nothing. I'm not interested and I'm not asking him anything."

"Okay, whatever you say."

As they reached the men Tami drew into Keaton's side and slid one arm under his jacket and around his waist. Kristin watched her brother, who'd never really shown a great deal of emotion, visibly melt at the arrival of his fiancée. The sight of the two of them caused a sharp prick of envy to stab sharply in her chest. She'd always wanted that—the kind of relationship that meant no matter where or when, you always had that person to count on. Someone to love you and someone you could love and trust with your heart, no matter what.

"The car is here," Jackson said, interrupting her longing. "Shall we go?"

"Yes. Good night, you two. Thanks for being great company."

She leaned forward and kissed Tami on the cheek,

and her brother, too. As she drew away she heard Tami whisper.

"Remember to ask him."

Kristin shook her head ever so slightly and turned away and walked beside Jackson to the car.

"What was that about?" Jackson asked.

"What was what about?"

"The 'ask him' thing."

Darn. He'd overheard. She made a dismissive gesture with her hand, then decided that deflection would be a waste of time. The man was used to cross-examining people who'd had far longer to think of something else to say than she did right now.

"Oh, that. Nothing, really. Tami just noticed that you had a tan line on your ring finger. She wanted me to ask you about your wife."

"My wife?"

He stopped in his tracks and Kristin was forced to stop with him. For a moment she saw a wealth of pain in his eyes, but then the anguish was replaced by a fierce expression—one that made her wish she'd held to her original plan to keep quiet.

"Yes, look, it's none of our business if you're divorced. Please, don't worry about it."

"I'm not divorced."

Kristin felt her mouth dry up and she swallowed hard. "You're not? Then—?"

"My wife is dead. And you're right. It is absolutely none of your business."

Ten

Kristin reeled with shock. It was one thing to think of Jackson as having been married but another to discover he was widowed. She'd blithely stomped over his feelings without thinking. She felt as if she was about two inches tall right now and she owed him a genuine apology.

"Oh, Jack. I'm so very sorry."

"Yeah," he said and looked away, his jaw a firm line of determination. "So am I. Let's go. I'll see you home."

They walked out of the venue and straight to the waiting car. The driver stood at the back door and handed Kristin into her seat and Jackson let himself in on the other side.

"To Ms. Richmond's apartment building first, please," Jackson said.

Beneath his directive, she could hear a note of weariness. Weariness, or maybe grief that she'd ripped open anew.

"Jack, I really am sorry. I had no idea."

"It's not something I shout from the rooftops, Kristin. Just drop it, okay? I'm not about to fall apart on you or anyone else. My wife's death and the months leading up to it were harrowing and are things I have no wish to rehash."

"Sure," she replied, feeling chastened. "If you ever need to talk, though, about anything, call me, okay?"

He looked across the darkened rear compartment of the car and she held his gaze, noting how his eyes glittered from the reflection of passing streetlights. Or was it emotion that made his eyes look like that?

"Thank you. But I'm fine. Truly. Now, about that question the reporter asked. We're possibly being paranoid but I have to ask, have you or anyone else in your family said anything to anyone about the new claim?"

She chose not to be offended that he would think that she might have let the information out.

She kept her voice level as she answered, "Our family is used to keeping things confidential. Especially things that might harm ourselves or the business. I think you can rest assured that none of us would have given anyone an inkling that there was another potential family skeleton rattling its bones."

"Hmm, then it's probably nothing to worry about."

"Well let's hope so. It wouldn't be unusual for a gossip columnist to make something up, though. Would we have a basis to sue if they did?"

"Depends on how they phrase it. Most of these gossip rags are based on conjecture and—" he made air quotes with his fingers "—information according to a source. And the trouble is, people believe that rubbish."

Kristin laughed at the absolute disgust in his tone. "Not a fan of the tabloids, then?"

He shook his head emphatically. "I'd rather read the latest spy thriller or sci-fi saga."

"Oh, I don't know, they provide a bit of light entertainment," she said to provoke him just a little.

"Not, I suspect, when it's your own family who's being featured."

She had to admit he had a point.

"Seriously, Kristin, these people make their money on other people's misery, and if they can't find the truth behind something, then they'll just go ahead and fabricate their own hideous lies."

There was so much bitterness behind his words. Kristin probed the wound.

"You sound as if you have experience in this?"

"I told you before about my parents. When the medical examiner's reports were released with the details of my parents' causes of death, our local paper had a field day. Nothing and no one was left alone. If people didn't want to give information, the paper started speculating about what our family life was really like behind closed doors. When it was revealed that my mother had injuries inconsistent with the car wreck and that my father had high levels of sedative in his blood, they began posing conjecture of spousal abuse in both directions. At that point I sought legal advice to shut them up. True or not, it was our business. Not the public's.

"But that was nothing compared to what my wife went through. Her first serious relationship fell apart rather spectacularly when she was in the early stages of her career, and because her lover was a man with a high profile, not to mention a wife she was unaware of, she was vilified by the press. It impacted her career greatly. She was a brilliant woman with a brilliant mind, and if she had lived, she could have gone all the way to the Supreme Court bench if she hadn't had that stain painted on her character."

Kristin listened carefully, hearing the words that remained unsaid. From what Jackson had just told her, his wife had to have been quite a bit older than him if her math and her limited knowledge of Supreme Court appointments was any indicator. She opted for a neutral response when every cell in her body writhed with curiosity and the need to know more.

"I can see why you feel the way you do. And again, I'm really sorry, Jackson. Sorry that my careless question raised a whole lot of past hurt for you, but especially sorry, too, for the hurt you sustained when your parents died. Losing one parent is hard enough, but losing two, together…" she shook her head slightly "…I just can't imagine what that must feel like, especially with no other family to support you."

He was silent for a time, then drew in a breath and slowly let it out. "Thank you. I'm sorry, it's a hot topic for me. You didn't need to hear all that."

"I'm glad you could tell me." She thought for a moment, then spoke before she could change her mind. "When we get to my apartment, would you like to come up for a while?"

"I thought you were tired, ready to call it a night."

"I'm tired, but I guess I'm not quite ready to be alone just yet. What do you say? I make a mean mug of cocoa."

"With marshmallows?"

"Of course."

He hesitated again and she would have bet her last week's salary that he was going to refuse, when he huffed out another short breath and nodded.

"Sure. But I'll make the cocoa. You always added too much sugar."

She laughed but felt that now familiar tug in her chest at the fact that he'd divulged yet another memory of their time together. Yet more proof that while he'd gone and left her, he'd never truly forgotten her any more than she'd forgotten him.

"I still do," she admitted. "Make sure you add plenty to my mug, okay?"

"Noted," he said with the beginnings of an answering smile.

When they reached her apartment building, he dismissed the driver with his thanks. As he escorted Kristin through the main doors, she nodded to the evening security guard. In the close confines of the elevator, she studied Jackson's reflection in the mirrored door. There were lines of strain around his eyes that hadn't been there earlier in the evening. Talking about his family and his late wife had obviously taken a toll. Cocoa was a good standby as a pick-me-up, but she doubted that it would give him the succor he looked like he needed right now.

When they arrived on her floor, they exited and walked down the carpeted corridor to her door. She pressed her forefinger on the print reader at her door to unlock it and ushered him inside.

"Kitchen is over to your right. You'll find everything you need there," she said. "I'm just going to emancipate my feet from these heels and I'll join you. Oh, and there's brandy in the cupboard beside the refrigerator if you want to add a dash of that to the cocoa."

She didn't wait for his response but crossed the living room to the short hallway that led to her bedroom. She sat on the bed and groaned as she slid her feet from the gold high-heeled pumps she'd worn with her gown. Should she change into something more comfortable, she wondered, or would that be too clichéd? She opted to remain dressed in her golden shimmer of a dress and, holding up the hem so she wouldn't catch her feet in it and fall flat on her face, she walked back into the living room.

"Find everything you need?" she called out to Jackson, whom she could see hovering in the kitchen.

"Just warming the milk," he said.

She realized he was watching a pot on the stove. "You can use the microwave, you know."

"When you're going to do something, you have to do it properly," he said firmly. "No shortcuts."

She'd always loved that about him. Loved his intensity and attention to detail. Especially when they'd made love. She derailed that train of thought the moment it thundered down the track. Regrettably, her body didn't get the signal, because a slow curl of desire uncoiled from deep inside her and sent a heated flush across her skin. She focused instead on perching on a breakfast barstool, and watched Jackson as he moved confidently around her kitchen. He added the cocoa, two spoons of sugar for her mug, then poured the steaming hot milk on top, stirring it and dressing it up with the mini marshmallows she kept in the pantry for exactly that purpose, but never got around to using herself.

His own, he kept unsweetened. Cocoa, hot milk and the bare minimum of marshmallows, that was it. No fuss, no frills. And he'd always been like that. Take his attire tonight, for example. Perfectly dressed in a simple tuxedo that couldn't have been cheap, but his cuff links were plain and unobtrusive and his shoes were good quality but not a statement of wealth or entitlement. His hair was groomed, without being in the latest, trendsetting style, but still managed to make him look elegant. With Jackson there was nothing out of place, but nothing unnecessary or extra to attract the eye, either. *Nothing except himself, that is*, she thought ruefully.

She hadn't been oblivious to the plentiful stares that came in his direction from women and men of all ages at the function tonight. He had that allure about him, made all the more captivating because he carried on as if he was completely oblivious to the attention he garnered. And, given the news she'd unwittingly drawn out of him regarding his marital status, it sounded as though he had good reason to be uninterested in other women. She wondered how long it was since he'd been widowed, but she didn't want to pry.

"Tonight went well, don't you think?" she said as they went over to her sitting room.

She curled up with her feet tucked underneath her on the couch and sipped her cocoa.

"It did. I understand from the treasurer that there were several pledges of ongoing support for the housing initiative. It's good to see money coming back into the community and giving people a helping hand."

A thought occurred to Kristin. "Would you be interested in visiting the latest development? I'm heading out there tomorrow for a cost management meeting with the building supervisor. Since you'll be handling the legal affairs for the foundation it might be a good opportunity for you to get an overview of what's happening on the ground."

"Let me check my calendar." He extracted his phone from his breast pocket, tapped the screen a few times and frowned. "No, it looks as though I'll be tied up all day."

Kristin told herself she felt relieved, and reminded herself that she shouldn't be seeking to spend more time with Jackson anyway. Even so, an unwarranted sense of disappointment pulled at her.

"No problem. Some other time, perhaps."

He nodded and took a long swig of his cocoa before putting his mug on the table and rising to his feet.

"I need to be on my way," he said abruptly. "No need to get up. I'll see myself out."

"No, no. I'll see you out," she protested, feeling another unreasonable pang of disappointment that he was leaving already.

She leaned forward and put her still half-full mug on the coffee table, and got her feet out from under her. But somewhere along the line, her feet tangled up in the hem of her dress, and despite her normally excellent sense of balance, she started to pitch forward. Jackson moved swiftly, catching her in his arms before she landed face-first onto the carpet. She did, however, end up chest-first against the solid wall of his body.

Her breasts crushed against him and his arms wrapped tight around her body. Through the satin of her gown, she felt the imprint of his fingers, the heat of his palms against her back. And, darn, she liked it. Her entire body flared in response, and she put her hands against the lapels of his jacket and started to push herself away. But the hands at her back didn't budge.

Kristin looked up into Jackson's fiercely glittering blue eyes, shocked by what she saw there. Passion. Heat. Disgust. All of those emotions warred for supremacy in the short time she stared into his eyes. And then she felt his hands move. Not away from her, but lower, to her buttocks.

A groan ripped from Jackson's throat before he

bent his face to hers and captured her lips. Shock coursed through her body at the long-missed and all too familiar touch of his mouth on hers. Shock and desire and a need to kiss him with all the pent-up frustration and sorrow she'd borne alone for far too long. He tasted of cocoa and the delicious tang that was innately his.

Jack's grip on her tightened as he pulled her lower body closer. The sensation of his arousal against her made her gasp as pleasure arrowed through her at the intimate touch. His kiss deepened, his tongue tasting her, sweeping her lips. His teeth grazed her lower lip as he pulled it into his mouth and sucked on the plump flesh.

This was everything she remembered and more. So much more. This wasn't the eager embrace of a boy; it was the demand of a man who knew what he wanted and just how much he was prepared to give to get it. A sense of desperation filled her, making her want to get closer, to feel more of him. To be rid of the trappings of civilized company and the formalities of the evening they'd spent together. To give in to the basic need they'd always aroused in each other.

And then, in an instant, it was over. Jackson shifted his hands to her upper arms and gently but deliberately pushed her away. She felt the loss of his physical imprint against her body like the loss of a limb.

"I shouldn't have done that," he said grimly, stepping farther away from her and pushing a hand through his hair.

"*We* shouldn't have done that. But we did," she

answered in a voice equally devoid of emotion. "But we're grown-ups. It doesn't have to mean anything. In fact, it doesn't mean anything."

He shot her a look that told her just how unconvincing she sounded. "You really believe what you just said? That it meant nothing?"

"It can't mean anything," she said firmly. "Can it?"

He stared at her in silence for a full twenty seconds before shaking his head slowly.

"No, it can't."

"And it doesn't have to make anything awkward. We've got it out of our system, right? It's not going to happen again."

"No. It is not." He said the words emphatically and his voice was filled with self-loathing. "I'm sorry."

"Jack, there's nothing to apologize for."

Kristin went to place a hand on his arm in reassurance but he took another step away.

"Good night," he said and stalked to the door.

She stayed rooted to the spot. Still in a state of disbelief at what had just happened between them. Her front door closed with a sharp click, and she sank onto the couch and tried to analyze why she felt so lost at his going. She'd told the truth when she said their kiss hadn't meant anything, hadn't she? Then why did she feel like she needed to hold herself back from racing to her door and down the hallway outside her apartment and begging him to return?

Eleven

At his desk the next morning, Jackson made notes automatically as the woman seated opposite him listed the litany of her husband's failings and why she was divorcing him. By the time she was done, and he escorted her to the door, he knew no amount of caffeine would fix the day ahead of him.

Last night had been a disaster from the moment he'd set eyes on Kristin. Keeping his hands off her should have been a simple matter of reminding himself what his purpose was in her life now and none of that purpose included kissing her like a man starved of, well, everything. He'd told himself that dancing with her at the charity gala was the worst thing he'd have to endure that night. The very fact he'd managed to hold her so lightly in his arms as they took their turn around the dance floor spoke volumes as to his restraint. So where was that restraint when it was time to leave her apartment after sharing cocoa with her? Why the hell had he given in to temptation and kissed her?

Sure, she'd literally fallen into his arms. Sure, she'd fit perfectly against his body the way she always had. But he hadn't needed to act on it. He was better than that, stronger than that, wasn't he? The entire night had been an exercise in torment as he battled the bittersweet memories of the times he'd attended similar functions with Annie and the last time he'd danced with her, and equally potent reminiscences of the last time he and Kristin had been together before his parents had died.

None of that gave him the right to allow impulse to overrule reason. And then there was Kristin's ability to diminish what they'd done with a select few words. *Nothing.* It had meant nothing to her. And dammit if that didn't piss him off. It shouldn't, obviously, but it did. And he hadn't been able to get her to budge from his thoughts since.

The girl from the front desk hailed him as he walked by.

"Another delivery for you," she said as she handed over the packet.

Jackson flipped it over. No name, and again a mailing office was used as the return address. He returned to his office and tore open the bag. Inside was a DNA report for an unnamed female and a printed note.

Dear Mr. Jones,
This report has been done at an independent
laboratory to help establish my connection to
the Richmond family. I trust you will be able
to compare my results with those of my sib-
lings and that this will expedite the matter of
the payment of what is due to me.

The note was unsigned.

Jackson composed another email to the claimant, stating he'd received the couriered DNA report and that it would take time to gather and then compare results. He was surprised to get an immediate reply.

The results are already in the Richmond family's pos-session. Last year they were all tested to prove Logan Parker was indeed the missing son. It shouldn't take you too long to compare the information already on hand with my own. My deadline stands.

Jackson leaned back in his chair and drummed the fingers of one hand on the desk. There was a knock at his door.

"Come in," he called.

Hector Ramirez entered and closed the door be-hind him. Jackson assessed the man's appearance quickly and found little to suggest that he had been unwell.

"That was a swift recovery," he commented as he gestured for Hector to take a seat.

"Ah, the power of love," Hector said enigmatically. "A great restorative to whatever ails a man. I take it last night went well?"

For a second, Jackson felt uncomfortable, but then he reminded himself that Hector was only expecting a report on the charity event. He filled his old friend in on the evening.

"And then you saw Kristin home?" Hector pressed.

"I did."

"And that was that."

Now Jackson knew something was up. "Hector, are you trying to matchmake?"

A ruddy flush of color stained the older man's cheeks. "I'm sorry, my friend. Guilty as charged. My partner in crime and soon-to-be partner in life sent me in here this morning for details because Kristin isn't taking any calls today."

Jackson filed the latter comment away for further examination and responded to Hector's admission of guilt with a shake of his head.

"Hector, you have my utmost respect, but it's too soon for me to be thinking about a new relationship. In fact, I don't know if I'll ever want to be with another person again. Losing Annie…"

His voice trailed off as his throat choked up and words failed him. But Hector wasn't to be deterred.

"Nancy told me that you and Kristin used to be an item. I guess we just thought that maybe the flame could be rekindled. Now we've found our own happiness, we just want the same for those we love. You can't blame us for that."

Jack barked a short laugh. So Kristin had told her

mother about them? He wondered how much information she'd disclosed. He knew she hadn't told her family anything about their relationship while they were going out. Back then, she'd been insistent about keeping things under wraps so her father wouldn't know that she was cheating on her promise to him not to have a boyfriend while she was in college. That had been fine with him. He hadn't wanted to add his family to the mix, either. They'd agreed, though, that after graduation they'd meet each other's family as they stepped out into their new life together. But then his family had ceased to exist and so had their relationship.

"I'd be grateful if you and Nancy would not try to interfere with Kristin and me," Jackson said in all seriousness.

"So there is hope?"

"No, there is no hope of rekindling anything. It's all water under the bridge. I take it as a win that we can at least work in a civil fashion with each other."

"So you broke her heart, then. I thought as much," Hector said with a wise expression in his eyes.

Jackson had no words. He had broken Kristin's heart. But even if he hadn't, would he want to pursue a relationship with her now? Like he'd said, the past couldn't be undone. He'd moved on, as had she.

"You know, Annie and I talked often, even up until the week before she passed away. It worried her that she was leaving you alone," Hector continued, filling the silence that had fallen between them. "She didn't want you to wallow after her death."

Jackson felt a prick of anger at his friend's words. "Wallow?" he said coldly.

Hector cocked his head to one side and looked at Jackson carefully. "Yes, that was the term she used and, no offense intended, I believe that is what you have been doing."

"Hector, as I said, it's too early for me to consider falling in love again, if ever. You can hardly talk. It's been fifteen years since your Mona passed. You didn't exactly rush into things again."

"But I was not alone. I have my children and now, to my greatest delight, I have another woman whom I love with all my heart. You are still young—you deserve a family, my friend. I only want what is best for you."

He pushed away the flare of hope that kindled deep inside at the thought of having a child with Kristin. Once upon a time, it had been his deepest wish to create a family with her, but no matter his confused feelings about her now, a family with Kristin was not in the cards.

"Thank you, but I'm not ready for any of that. I went into marriage with Annie with my eyes wide open and a sure knowledge that we wouldn't have a family together even if we wanted one. I can't imagine wanting that with anyone else. Now, can we discuss some business?"

"Certainly, it's what I'm here for after all. No more of this social chitchat," Hector said with a teasing glint in his eyes.

And they did get down to business, but all through

it, Jackson couldn't stop thinking about the fact that Annie had obviously discussed him with Hector in the lead-up to her death. But she hadn't left him completely alone. She'd left him with full responsibility for Ben's care, and he'd promised that come what may he'd be there for him. No matter what. And that meant not clouding his emotions with anyone else. Already his work had gotten in the way last night and Jack promised himself that would not happen again. He would not let Annie down or sully her memory by reneging on his promise to her to always be there for her son. There was no room in his life for another person, especially not Kristin Richmond, whatever his subconscious kept telling him.

Jackson entered the offices of Richmond Developments the following Monday morning, with his agenda for the meeting at the forefront of his mind. The fact he was seeing Kristin again had nothing to do with his brisk pace, he told himself as he followed one of the receptionists to the meeting room that had been set aside for them. Nor did it have anything to do with not being able to get thoughts of her to budge from his mind ever since his conversation with Hector. *Who the hell are you kidding?* a little voice in the back of his mind jeered as he entered the room and instantly looked for her.

He was pleased to note that Logan and Keaton were already there, with Honor and Tami arriving soon behind him. Next were Hector and Nancy. Which only left Kristin still to arrive.

"Shall I start the video link with the others?" Keaton said as they all took seats around the table, which faced a large TV screen at the end of the room.

"Sure," Jackson said. "We'll wait five more minutes for Kristin, but then we'll have to commence. I have another appointment at my office in an hour."

"Perhaps I should go and find her," Nancy said, rising from her chair.

"No need, Mom," Kristin said as she breezed into the meeting room. "Sorry I'm a little late."

Jackson noted that she walked past the first empty chair in the room, next to his own, and went and sat between her mom and Logan. Had she deliberately arrived late so she wouldn't have to risk being alone with him? He firmed his lips. That was fine. He could live with that. In fact, it was what he wanted, wasn't it? A professional relationship. That was all.

But even though he belabored the point in his thoughts, he couldn't help but let his gaze rake her body. She'd worn her lustrous blond hair loose today, and her makeup was minimal compared to the femme fatale look she'd worn to their dinner together or the glamour she'd exuded for the gala. She was beautiful, no matter how she presented herself, and the carefully cut red suit she wore today screamed corporate chic. The fine wool two-piece fitted her perfectly and accentuated the swell of her breasts beneath a cream-colored lace-edged camisole. The jacket nipped in securely at the narrow curve of her waist.

He realized he was staring and looked away, but

not before he'd noted the slightly smug smile on Hector's face. It didn't make any difference, he thought defiantly. A man would have to be completely blind not to find Kristin Richmond thoroughly appealing, and he most definitely was not blind. He was also not interested. *Sure you're not*, that little voice interrupted again. Okay, fine, if he were totally honest with himself, he'd never stopped being interested in Kristin. But being interested was different from taking things further, and right now he had work to do.

The heirs from the Virginia-based family came on screen, seated in a similar meeting room as the Seattle Richmonds. Not for the first time, Jackson wondered about the man who'd set up mirror lives on two different coasts. How on earth had he juggled everything and expected to get away with it? Then again, he had gotten away with it for over thirty years. Anyway, that wasn't his concern right now. He called the meeting to order and explained about the forensic assessment of the photographs.

"So, as you will see by the copies of the report from the analyst, these pictures do not appear to have been altered. Given the data that we have gone through from your staff records here, we believe the woman in question was Jenna Emerson. I've engaged an investigator to follow that trail with a request for privacy and urgency."

"I remember Jenna," Nancy said. "She was a sweet young woman. She worked in the general secretarial pool and stood in for Stella, Douglas's PA, while Stella took an extended leave of absence when her father was ill. So he had an affair with her, too?"

"We don't know that for certain yet, Mom," Kristin hurried to assure her mother, who sounded shell-shocked.

"That's right, Nancy. We have not been able to substantiate any of this person's claims to date. Which leads me to the latest development."

He quickly explained the DNA report he'd received in the post.

"We would require testing of all of you for comparative purposes."

Keaton shook his head.

"We went through all that this time last year when Logan arrived. Surely the data from that will be sufficient."

"It's interesting you mention that," Jack said. "Because the claimant seemed to know it also. They said that their independent report should be compared to the data collected from all of you last year."

"But how would they know about it?" Logan asked, incredulous.

"Perhaps Douglas was still involved with Jenna at that time," Nancy said faintly. "Nothing would surprise me anymore. Until Douglas's funeral, we had no idea about Eleanor, so it's entirely possible he kept Jenna on a string, too. He might have said something to her about Logan's return to the family."

"Mom, we all know that if Dad really was this person's father, he would have made greater financial accommodation for them and their mom. He might have been a bastard but he was a fair bastard when it came to providing for his kids. That hundred thousand dollars looks more like a payoff, to me. Not support," Keaton said.

"But how can we be sure he didn't?" Nancy said, her voice sounding utterly weary of it all.

"There has to be something. Some financial record somewhere," Lisa said on screen.

"What date did this Jenna woman leave your employment?" Fletcher asked. "We can get a search done of the company accounting here for around that period and see if there are any discrepancies. Who knows what Dad was able to hide before the accounting systems became tighter? There are print and digital records of that period. I'll put one of our best accountants on it."

"Thank you, Fletcher," Logan said, "And Kristin, will you do the same here?"

"You bet I will," Kristin said with determination.

Jackson thanked everyone for their cooperation and drew the meeting to a close. The TV screen went blank, and everyone began to file out of the room. Jackson moved to cut Kristin off from leaving the room straight away.

"A word with you, if you don't mind?" he queried lightly.

He felt the huff of frustration she uttered, but she nodded and stepped away from him, crossing her arms and staring at him with a challenge clear in her eyes.

"What is it? I have work to do, and I believe we're under some urgency after today's discussion."

"We are, but this is important, too. I need to talk to you about last Thursday night."

"I thought we agreed there was nothing to talk about," she said with those arms still firmly crossed and her eyes alight with a burning fire.

"We both know that's not true. Kissing you like that was..."

"What? Wrong? Yes, it was. It was very wrong, and we've agreed that nothing will come from it. I have reservations about trusting you, and you clearly don't want to make another commitment. I'm good with that. Now, can I get to work, or do you want to rehash this some more?"

She was hurting. He could see it in every line of her body language and in the tone of her voice.

"I'm sorry, Kristin. For the past, for the present, for everything."

"Yeah, I believe you've said something along those lines before. Look, we have a past. I think we're ready to move on. So, can we shelve all this postmortem rubbish over what was simply an impulse and leave it there?"

A spark of irritation burned deep in his mind. That impulse had led to a kiss that continued to haunt him—awake or asleep. And despite everything, he wanted more. But she was making it fervently clear that was not going to happen. She had been completely correct in her statement that he wasn't open to another commitment. But was he completely averse to a dalliance? A simple outlet of physical and emotional frustration? Could they consider exploring that without the complication of putting a label on what they did and who they were while they were doing it?

Before he could overthink it, he started to speak. "It was more than an impulse, Kristin. I think we both know it. And I think we still have something going between us. What we do with it is up to us. The way I see it, we have two options. One, we continue to try to ignore this awareness between us or, two, we act on it. We don't need to have any strings attached, but maybe we owe it to ourselves to give in, even just once, and get this out of the way once and for all."

Stunned surprise froze her features, and he could see her mentally processing his words. Her pupils had dilated slightly, and her breathing quickened. The pulse, visible at the base of her slender throat, beat more rapidly.

"You're suggesting a fling?"

"How about friends with benefits?"

"We are not friends."

"But we could be. After all, we know each other well enough, and last Thursday night's kiss proved we are still fiercely compatible."

She looked as if she wanted to argue with him on that point for just a moment, but then her arms dropped to her sides.

"Let me think about it," she said stiffly.

He let go of the breath he'd been holding, surprised and satisfied she hadn't rejected his suggestion out of hand.

"I still don't fully trust you," she said obstinately.

"And you don't have to," he replied gently. "But maybe we can work on the trust issue while we explore our…friendship."

"I'll get back to you on that," she said.

With that, she abruptly turned and left the meeting room. Jackson began to gather his papers up from the table and realized his hands were shaking slightly. Anticipation for what might come? he wondered. Or fear that she would turn him down? He hoped it was the former and knew, without a shadow of a doubt, that they needed to do this. They needed, more than anything, to lay to rest the ghosts of the past.

And his love for Annie, his promises to her? They would still be safely under lock and key in his heart. This thing with Kristin, if it went ahead, would be purely physical. He could deal with that. It was the emotional commitment he refused to accept.

Because, when it came to emotions, he was all wrung out. And he suspected Kristin was, too. But what was friendship, if not an emotional commitment? Had he just made the second biggest mistake of his life?

Twelve

Kristin paced the floor of her apartment. Tonight she was expected at her mom's for a Christmas Eve get together. She knew that Nancy had asked Jackson to join them and that he'd accepted. She really didn't know how she felt about that. But then again, nothing in life was as it had been. It was just over a year since her father had died, and their entire world had turned upside down and inside out. And it didn't look as if things were going to get better anytime soon.

On the bright side, if it could be called that, both Fletcher's accounting team and her own had found evidence of two payments of fifty thousand dollars each to an unknown creditor just over twenty-five years ago. Further investigation had revealed the recipient to be Jenna Emerson. The dates tied in with the time she left Richmond Developments and were near enough to the age of Douglas's supposed love child. How the accounting teams at both Richmond Developments and Richmond Construction had never questioned the payments at the time bore serious scrutiny. Kristin had authorized a historical audit to make sure there were no other skeletons about to come out of her fiscal closet. The one security she had now was that the systems she had in place at Richmond Developments allowed no bogus invoices to make it through.

But the trail back to Jenna Emerson made it begin to look more and more as if the person had a legitimate claim—which raised the question, why, if their claim was legitimate, had they used such underhanded means to stake it? She only hoped that the results of the DNA comparisons would give them the truth, once and for all.

On her coffee table, Kristin's phone buzzed to alert her to an incoming message. She snatched up her phone and tapped the screen. It was from Jackson.

Need a ride to your mom's tonight?

She chewed her lower lip before answering. She hadn't given him a response yet regarding the preposterous suggestion he'd made last Monday, but it had never been far from her mind. She'd almost hoped he'd tell her he'd changed his mind, but he'd kept radio silence since that discussion in the meeting room.

Kristin didn't want to examine too closely how his suggestion had made her feel. The moment the words had passed his lips her entire body had begun to heat and her heart rate increase in anticipation of what might happen next.

What this it? Was this what happened next? She'd accept his offer of a ride, they'd make nice and polite at her mom's Christmas Eve gathering, and then they'd race to his place, or hers, for crazy monkey sex and hope to get it out of their systems?

A swell of desire poured through her, heating her body anew and making her body tense with anticipation. And there, she admitted, was her answer. She desired him. No matter how much she distrusted him in personal matters, he'd been faultless in his handling of the love child issue so far. And worse, she had never quite lost that physical recognition every time they were in the same room. There really was only one answer she could give him, but she thought it might be fun to let him sweat it a little longer. For now, she'd accept his offer of a ride. What happened next, well, she'd play that by ear.

Yes, please. I'll be downstairs at seven, she replied.

I'll be there, came the immediate response.

Suddenly it became more important than ever that she look her best tonight. She had about half an hour before he'd be here. Kristin strode to her bedroom and opened her lingerie drawer, her hand settling on a bright red lace and satin bodysuit that she'd bought on a whim and yet never worn. It was the kind of sexy bit of something someone wore purely to titillate.

She lifted it from the drawer and imagined Jackson's face when he saw it. Whoa, there! She cautioned herself. *When?* Maybe it should be *if.* Either way, her body hummed with anticipation at the thought. She quickly shucked off the eminently sensible black trousers she was wearing, together with the high-necked ruby-red cashmere sweater she'd teamed with it, and slipped off her bra and panties. Taking a deep breath she donned the bodysuit, the hook-and-eye fasteners giving her a bit of trouble at first, but she conquered them and slowly turned and looked at herself in her full-length mirror.

She studied her reflection with a critical eye, turning this way and that before nodding at herself in the mirror. It would do. The garment hugged the curves of her bottom perfectly. And the satin back was silky soft to the touch. She shivered a little and not because it was cold. Feeling brave, she slipped on a pair of black stiletto pumps and posed, thrusting one hip out, hands on her hips. Yeah, she looked bad-ass. Better yet, she felt it, too.

Without immediately putting her other clothes back on, Kristin went to her bathroom. She added to the makeup she'd already done for this evening, making her eyes look smokier and applying a couple of extra layers of mascara for good measure. Then, she slicked on the red lipstick that she'd noticed caught Jackson's attention. She smiled at her reflection, satisfied with the end result. She redressed in the pants and sweater and put on a black leather jacket to complete her ensemble.

If she went through with this, she would knock Jackson's socks off. She made a sound of disgust. Who was she kidding? From the minute he'd suggested his ridiculous friends-with-benefits proposal, she'd been interested. Thinking about it had tormented her ever since. It was easier to outright hate him. But then he'd kissed her and awakened all sorts of feelings she'd thought were tucked away forever.

Feelings she didn't want to put under a microscope.

Maybe he was right. Maybe they could do this strictly physically and it would resolve both her still-simmering anger toward him and their attraction to each other. It would save a lot of stress and heartache, that was for sure.

Kristin looked at her watch. It was almost time for Jack to collect her. She went downstairs and looked out the foyer doors just as he pulled up in the pick-up zone. Perfect timing. But then again, timing had never been his problem.

She wondered what his wife had been like. What kind of woman had been capable of capturing and holding Jackson Jones? And with that thought, Kristin realized where a whole lot of her old hurts had sprung from. She hadn't been able to hold on to him. In fact, when the chips were down, he hadn't even told her what the problem was. He'd simply left. For all these years, she'd blamed herself for that and been mad as hell at him for letting her down. So, what could she have done differently? Anything? Nothing? She made a sound of disgust and walked toward his waiting car, determined to once again leave the past where it belonged. Buried. Not to be brought out and chewed over. Not to be used as a mirror for her failings.

"Bad day?" Jackson asked as she settled herself in the passenger seat.

"No, why?"

"You look angry."

She shook her head. "Just letting some things get on top of me. That's all. It's a tough time of year, what with the anniversary of Dad's death and everything," she said, not entirely untruthfully.

"Anything I can help you with?"

"Maybe later," she said with a small smile. "I'll let you know."

"I'm here if you need me," he said as he headed for the interstate that would take them to Nancy's home.

She fought back the urge to snort at his comment. There if she needed him? At the time she'd most needed him, as they were about to graduate together and begin a future together, he'd disappeared. But she needed to move on. To accept that she wasn't the same person she was back then, and neither, most likely, was he. They'd both grown and changed in the intervening years, and banging that old drum would just keep her locked firmly in the past. She didn't want to be that person anymore.

Her reluctance to trust anyone after Jack had led to her making poor choices with relationships. And her distrust had seen most men walk away in the end. With the exception of Isaac, of course, who'd been led away in handcuffs. She'd thought she knew him through working with him so closely. She'd truly thought he had her back and was someone she could look forward to a future with and instead, he'd been holding a knife to her back the whole time. Faking his affection for her while he fed sensitive financial information to their main competitor. Discovering his deceit so soon after the shock of her father's duplicity had made her doubt her ability to read anyone properly. It was easier not to get involved. Period. But if she'd had the chance to understand why Jackson had left her in the first place, would that have changed anything? She wanted to think so.

"You still have that angry look on your face. Are you sure you're okay?" Jackson asked, interrupting her reverie.

She gave him an apologetic look. "I'm sorry, yeah, I'm fine. I'm looking forward to a break from work, although I know it'll keep worrying at the back of my mind."

"It's not easy to switch off, especially when your job is such an integral part of who you are."

She looked at him in surprise. Many of the men she'd associated with didn't see her career as being as important a part of her life as their jobs were to them. It was a patriarchal and outdated viewpoint, and she'd found it easier to simply ignore them and carry on doing what she did best.

"And is your work an integral part of who you are,

now?" she asked, suddenly curious to learn more about him.

"Definitely, but I've had to train myself not to bring my work home. And, you might laugh, but I've found meditation useful as a tool to switch between work mode and home mode."

"You? Meditation?"

He laughed. "Yeah, I know. Back in the day I was too busy rushing from one thing to the next to even consider something like that, but it gives your mind peace and allows separation. If anything, it gives me perspective on things."

"I need some of that."

For the rest of their journey, they discussed the techniques he used. It was only as they turned into the gate at Nancy's house that it occurred to Kristin to ask him what had made him turn to meditation in the first place.

"I guess it was a turning point in my career as a litigator. I was bringing work home every day and was struggling with a challenging case. Annie had obviously reached the end of her tether with me and my foul moods and insisted I try meditation before I developed an ulcer or had a heart attack from stress. She coached me for the first week or so, and after that it came naturally to me."

"She sounds like she was a strong woman to take you on in a bad mood."

Jackson cocked a brow and shot her a cheeky look. "Are you saying I'm not nice in a temper?"

She laughed. "I don't know anyone who is. If I

remember correctly, when you were in a temper, everyone but your most staunch professor managed to make themselves unavailable."

He uttered a cynical laugh. "Yeah, that's true. I didn't like myself much when I was like that. I had a lot of repressed anger around my upbringing."

"I'm sorry. I didn't mean to bring that up."

"No, it's okay. I can talk about it now. Another thing Annie insisted on and which I fought her on until I realized she was prepared to walk out on me if I didn't take that step, is that I sought counseling to unravel my feelings about my parents and their deaths. I wish I'd done it sooner but—" he shrugged "—life is what it is. Sometimes we have to complete the journey to be a better person in the long run."

It was such a philosophical viewpoint—and totally unexpected from the man sitting next to her—that it left Kristin speechless. There were depths to Jack that she'd never seen before. Depths she was intrigued to know more about. Depths that most couples would explore during pillow talk.

She squirmed a little in her seat, the lace of her teddy lightly abrading her nipples and making her suddenly all too aware of where she'd decided this night would end.

"The journeys aren't always pleasant ones," she said as she reached for her door handle.

"No, but if we can learn from them, then they were worth the pain."

He put out a hand and stopped her from immediately exiting the car. "Kristin, before we go in, can you tell me if you've thought any further about my suggestion?"

It was all she'd been able to think about. Her body flamed to life, aching for more than the press of fabric on skin and for far, far more than the touch of his hand on hers.

"Yes," she said emphatically. "I have."

"And may I know your answer?"

She lifted her gaze to his and stared straight into his eyes. "Yes. My answer is yes."

He blew out a breath, and there was a glint of anticipation in his eyes. "Thank you. So, how shall we do this? By appointment? Days ending in Y?"

Kristin laughed, delighted that he could lighten such a serious prospect with a touch of the humor she'd loved. Humor she'd seen very little of since he'd reentered her life.

"How about we start with tonight and then play it by ear. After all, once might be enough."

One side of his mouth quirked upward in a challenging smile. "Do you really think once will be enough?"

"We'll have to see, won't we?"

Kristin turned away and alighted from the car and heard him do the same. He joined her in the portico by the front door, standing close, but not close enough to touch. Even so, she felt the tension that poured off him in waves. A tension she knew her body reflected.

"Not a word to anyone, though," he said.

"Oh, absolutely," she agreed. "This is between you and me, for as long as it lasts. No regrets."

"No regrets," he echoed as Martha opened the front door to them and welcomed them inside.

As she crossed the threshold to her childhood home, Kristin felt a thrill of expectancy that she hadn't felt in a very long time. A spark of hope she hadn't allowed herself to feel since all the negative impacts she and her family had endured this past year. Maybe tonight would see a new beginning. And, she thought with a private smile as she joined her family in the main salon, maybe this friends-with-benefits arrangement would be just what she needed to let go of her past hurts and disappointments and to live the life she truly wanted.

Thirteen

Jackson kept an eye on the time with irritating regularity. It wasn't that the evening wasn't truly lovely. In fact, it was better than that. It was a celebration of family and it was the kind of thing that he'd heard about but never fully understood. His own parents had always been busy on the social scene. From an early age he'd be left at home with a sitter while they attended one function or another. They'd come home either so wrapped up in each other that they couldn't even see the little boy waiting for them on the landing upstairs or seething with fury at each other for some imagined slight or hint of infidelity.

Once he'd processed his feelings about his upbringing he'd learned to let go of his confusion and resentment about the relationship his parents had

had. Jack took a sip of the whiskey he'd been nursing for the past hour and observed the people around him. A tight-knit family unit who'd seen fit to include him in their group and in the announcement of Keaton and Tami's engagement. It was a Christmas Eve like no other that he'd experienced before, and it was about to become even more different when he and Kristin left.

He glanced again at his watch. The hands had barely moved. It wasn't that he was desperate to leave the gathering. Oh, hell, of course he was. After the bombshell of an answer Kristin had given him in the car, he wanted to lock the doors and drive them both straight to his place and explore exactly where the night would take them. Had he been the younger, more impulsive version of himself, he probably would have done just that. But the more mature and stable man he was today realized that savoring the expectation of what he and Kristin would share tonight was part of the journey to being together.

He only hoped it wouldn't mess everything up between them professionally. But that would only happen if emotions became entangled, and they were both clear on that score. This was to be a release of sorts. A mutual and entirely adult way to deal with the simmering tension that hovered between them every single time they were within ten feet of each other. Hell, even more than ten feet, he realized as he watched her animatedly talking with Honor by the massive Christmas tree that had pride of place in the bay window facing the front lawn.

"Can I get you another drink?" Keaton said from beside him.

"No, thank you. Just the one for me tonight. I'm driving."

"I saw you and Kristin arrive together."

"Is there a problem?"

Keaton eyed him carefully. "Well, that all depends on why."

"I offered her a ride. She accepted."

Kristin's brother came straight to the point. "Have you got designs on my sister?"

Jackson remained calm. Not an easy feat, given what he planned to do with Kristin later this evening.

"She's a beautiful woman. I'm just appreciating the view."

Keaton gave him another hard look. "She puts on a good front, Jackson, but she's vulnerable. Don't mess with her, okay?"

"Is this a directive from a caring older brother?" Jack asked with what he hoped was just the right amount of self-possession.

"You could say that. She's borne more than her fair share in the past year and takes things very personally when they go wrong. It's just the way she is. She doesn't always show it, but deep down she can be as fragile as spun glass. Bear that in mind, okay?"

"Your sister's heart is quite safe from me," Jackson said firmly.

Keaton gave him a short, sharp nod. "Good to hear. Because we've been happy with your handling of the claim on Dad's estate, and I'd hate to have to fire you."

While there was an element of humor in the other man's tone, Jack could see he was still deadly serious. The message was crystal clear. Step out of line and step straight out the door.

"Duly noted," he replied.

It didn't make him take his eyes off Kristin, however. She looked more animated tonight than he'd seen her recently. There was a glow about her that he found infinitely appealing. The sweater she wore fit loosely but skimmed her breasts and hips, leaving a man in no doubt whatsoever that she had curves beneath the fine wool. And her trousers were cut to fit her elegant, long legs to perfection. He remembered the sensation of those legs wrapped around his waist and felt a deep, dragging pull of desire.

Kristin looked across to him at that moment, and their eyes met. Did she know he was thinking of her naked in his bed? A light touch of color bloomed on her cheeks, and she raised her glass to him in a silent toast before turning her attention back to her conversation. His view of her was blocked by Martha, who was taking a tray of canapés around the room. How much longer would the torment of waiting last?

Another hour, it turned out. But finally he and Kristin were, with the others, saying their goodbyes and heading out to their cars. A heavy rain fell, which thankfully made lingering farewells impossible. A sense of urgency gripped him. All he wanted to do was get Kristin back to his place before she changed her mind.

Beside him, Kristin sighed happily. "That was a nice evening."

"They're not always?" he asked, casting her a glance.

"Well, the last one at my mother's house certainly wasn't," she said on a laugh. "At least I managed to curb my drinking tonight."

"And at least I wasn't lined up in your sights tonight."

"Oh, you're lined up in my sights. Just not the same way as three weeks ago."

With those words, he knew she wasn't changing her mind. His fingers tightened on the steering wheel, and he forced himself to relax and focus on his driving. The last thing he wanted to do was jeopardize what was promising to be a very good evening, indeed. That said, he was relieved when he pulled up in his parking bay at Eastlake.

"Wait here while I grab an umbrella."

"I didn't know you lived in one of the houses *on* the lake," Kristin said, peering through the darkness and the rain. "Do they rock?"

He laughed. "Not that I noticed. And it's plumbed into public water so it's quite civilized. Besides, I figured if I was going to move here, I might as well take full advantage of the water. Hang on, I'll be right back."

He left the car, extricated a large umbrella from the trunk and held the door open for Kristin. He put his free arm around her waist and held her lightly as they traversed the wooden pathways through the homes built on the water. They were at his two-story home with what looked like an open upper deck in minutes, but even so the cold night air had permeated his coat. Judging by the occasional shiver he felt coming from Kristin, it had cut through her leather jacket, too.

Once inside, he helped her out of her jacket and hung it and his coat on the rack at the front door.

"Can I offer you a drink?" he asked as he led her farther into the bottom level of the house.

"Something to warm me up would be nice."

"Some mulled wine, or, hang on, I have a better idea. You're chilled to the bone, aren't you?"

"Kind of, but it's nice and warm in here. I'll be fine. Wine sounds lovely."

He had radiant heat throughout the property, but even so, he knew how to warm her up faster than that.

"Come upstairs with me," he said with a grin and held out his hand.

She took it, and he felt a delicious prickle of awareness trickle up his arm at her touch. It made him realize just how little they'd touched in the past four weeks. But that was all about to change tonight. As they walked upstairs, she looked around, spying the additional staircase that led to the next floor.

"Just how big is this place?" she asked curiously.

"Twenty-two hundred square feet, give or take."

"That's pretty sizable for a man on his own, isn't it?"

"It fits my purposes," he answered noncommittally.

"Do you have a boat berth, as well?"

"Two, actually," he admitted.

"And two boats?"

"Just the one, but it's in a dry stack over winter. I'll retrieve it come spring."

Kristin halted in her step and looked at him carefully.

"There is so much I don't know about you," she said softly.

"Anything you want to know, just ask," he said simply and led the way to the master suite and into the master bathroom. She gasped in delight when she saw the oversize spa bath. At one end was a massive picture window framing the glittering lights of nearby floating homes and buildings on the other side of the lake.

"Wow, so beautiful," she said, stepping forward for a closer look.

"It is," he agreed. "The glass is privacy tinted."

"How decadent," she said with a gurgle of laughter. "So, after a hard day at work, you can lie here in the evening with your favorite beverage and stare out at the lake."

"I could, but I haven't. But we can amend that situation tonight if you'd like."

He took a step closer behind her. The scent of her perfume wafted gently around him as if enticing him to shift the swath of hair at her nape and push it aside so he could place his lips right there.

"What? Now?"

"We're both cold, aren't we?"

She gave him a smile that made her eyes light up with a wicked gleam. "So, no mulled wine?"

He laughed. "I can get the mulled wine and bring it up. Why don't you run the bath?"

"Just regular wine is fine, or champagne if you have it."

"I do. And champagne it is. We can celebrate putting our differences aside."

"I like the sound of that," she said and bent over to turn on the faucet.

Jackson took a moment to admire the view of her bottom snugly outlined by the fabric of her trousers before tearing his gaze away and heading downstairs. It only took a moment to gather up a bottle of champagne from his wine fridge and two crystal flutes, and he was back. She was still fully dressed, and he wasn't sure whether to feel sorry about that or to savor the anticipation of undressing her himself. Opting for the latter, he swiftly popped the cork on the bottle and filled the flutes with the sparkling wine.

The bath was slowly filling, and Kristin sat on the edge with one hand trailing in the water.

"How hot do you like it?" she asked, her voice rich with double entendre.

"As hot as you can stand," he said with a slow smile.

He handed her a flute and raised his in a toast. "To friends with benefits," he said.

She rose to her feet and clinked her glass with his. "I'll drink to that."

They sipped their wine. Then Jackson took her glass and put both to one side of the bath.

"We're wearing too many clothes," he murmured, stepping forward and putting his hands on the hem of her sweater.

"Always so observant," she teased as he began to lift the sweater.

Jackson spied the bodysuit and felt a rush of blood to his head at the sight. He couldn't wait to uncover more of it. It only took seconds to divest her of the sweater, and then his hands were at the zipper and fastener of her pants. A light swoosh of sound left them pooling around her feet. Kristin stepped out of the trousers and kicked the fabric to one side, standing in her high-heeled pumps, hands on hips, feet slightly apart and sheer temptation painted all over her.

"You look…" Words failed him.

Beneath the red satin and lace of her bodysuit, her creamy skin glowed with vitality. Her breasts swelled in the lacy cups, and through the material he could see the darker skin of her nipples. Nipples that had drawn into tight buds. He reached out one hand.

"May I?"

She nodded, her eyes not straying from his for a second.

Jackson cupped one breast and let his thumb trace the outline of the peak of her nipple. A low hiss escaped her at his touch, and a tremor shuddered through her body.

"Still cold?" he asked.

"Warming up by the second," she said through gritted teeth.

He smiled and cupped her other breast as well and repeated the action. "How about now?"

"Getting there," she answered huskily.

Her eyes glittered like shards of slate as he stroked her through the lace. It was intoxicating looking at her like this and, he noticed, she hadn't lost any sensitivity of her nipples. In fact, if he kept this up and added a little something extra, he'd be able to coax her to climax right here. Bending his head and taking one nipple into his lips, through the lace, he added that something extra.

With one arm hooked around her waist, he kept playing the other nipple with his fingers while his tongue swirled against the rough lace and her taut bud, letting the rhythm and the pressure of his tongue become his sole focus. Well, that and the way her body began to tremble against him. She moaned a protest when he pulled his mouth away briefly so he could pull down her shoulder strap and peel the cup away from her tender skin.

Her fingers drove into his hair and dug into his scalp, pulling him to her breast and he readily obliged, this time taking her nipple fully into his mouth and suckling hard. She gasped beneath the determined onslaught, and he felt her entire body tense before jerking in his arms as her climax took her over the edge. Her long legs buckled, and Jackson supported her weight as he gentled his actions and drew away from her. He sat on the tiled edge of the bath and pulled her into his lap, burying his face in the curve of her neck and plying her with small kisses that worked their way to her lips.

She kissed him back with equal intensity, her hands still tangled in his hair and her body still trembling from the power of her orgasm.

"Okay?" he asked.

"More than okay," she answered. "It seems you can still play me like a virtuoso. Now let's see if I can return the favor."

"I look forward to it, but first, the bath. I think we could do with the soak, right?"

She lowered her eyelids. He could see she was planning something—and his body reacted instantly, his erection straining against his boxer briefs—but she nodded and leaned past him to turn off the faucet before standing and shimmying out of the bodysuit. She'd looked magnificent in the red concoction, but naked, she looked even more so. Jackson drew in a long breath as he let his eyes rake over her body. A light flush of color stained her skin and she no longer shivered with cold. Mission accomplished in that regard, he thought with satisfaction, but only his first mission, he reminded himself. And hopefully the first of many tonight.

"Stand up and let me undress you," Kristin commanded.

He did as she asked and she wasted no time in unbuttoning his shirt and tugging it free from his trousers. Her hands skimmed over his shoulders, his chest and lower to the waistband of his pants. She deftly loosened his belt and unsnapped the fastener, before sliding his zipper down slowly. Her hand slipped inside his trousers, her fingers skimming then wrapping around the aching length of his erection through the fabric of his briefs.

"Pretty warm, here," she teasingly murmured against his lips.

"You have that effect on me," he admitted, his voice a little strained now as desire pounded in his veins.

She'd always affected him more than any other woman he'd ever met. He'd only ever had to catch a glimpse of her to crave her. And the view she presented to him now escalated craving into an all-consuming hunger.

Kristin pushed his trousers to the floor then slowly removed his boxer briefs. His swollen arousal sprang free, and she was quick to take him in her hands again. The sensation of warm skin against skin made him groan in appreciation. She slid her hand up and down slowly, increasing the pressure of her hold and releasing it, driving him slowly insane with lust while she did so. And then she bent to her knees.

"Kristin, no. Not yet," he growled.

But it was too late. She looked up at him as she took him into her mouth and it was all he could do not to fist his hands in her hair as she closed her lips around him, drawing him deeper into the wet, hot cavern of her mouth. He tried his best not to lose it, even resorting to mentally reciting the alphabet backward, but she had tricks that drove him to utter distraction. And when her tongue and lips and the pressure of her mouth sent him soaring, he could do nothing more than allow it to happen, giving in to the pleasure she gave him.

They finally made it into the bath, their clothes in a heap on the bathroom floor and their bodies humming with satisfaction as they sank together into the warm water. Kristin had twisted her hair up and secured it into a knot at the top of her head. Tendrils of hair escaped the loose confinement and curled softly around her face and neck in the steam that rose from the bath.

"That was nice," Kristin said, taking her flute from the side of the bath and having a sip of her wine.

"Nice?" Jack said with a cocked eyebrow.

She laughed. "Okay, it was better than nice."

"Good. I'd hate to think I'd lost my touch."

"Oh, you haven't lost anything," she said in reply.

He drank a little wine and then reached for the bottle of bathing gel that stood on the side of the bath. He poured a little into his hands and beckoned for her to come over to him.

"Turn around," he suggested. "Let me do your back."

She moved slowly through the bath and did as he said, perching between his legs. The sensation of her buttocks against his most sensitive part made him harden again. She noticed it, too, and wriggled slightly.

"Behave," he admonished lightly, enjoying the lightheartedness of being together with her again.

"Just getting comfortable," she said innocently.

"While I am not," he said on a laugh.

"Sorry," she said in a voice that implied she was anything but.

He laughed again and began to apply his soapy hands to her skin, smoothing them across her shoulders and down her arms before doing the same along her spine. Her skin felt soft and supple beneath his touch, but he could feel her ribs through her skin as he gently massaged her. She never used to be quite this thin, he thought, casting his mind to their past. Was her weight loss deliberate, he wondered, or had the stress of the past year been an influencing factor? Whatever it was, it piqued concern in him. She'd always been slender but she was even more so now.

He slid his hands up her shoulders and, sensing the tension she held there, he firmly massaged the knots away.

"That feels amazing. You have incredible hands," she murmured, dropping her head forward.

"You're welcome."

He shifted his hands, lightening the strokes until he was skimming her shoulders and back in long strokes again, every now and then slipping under her arms to brush the sides of her breasts. And then, because he couldn't resist her any longer, he allowed himself to cup her breasts again and to play with her nipples with hands still slick with soap.

Beneath his touch she moaned with pleasure and he leaned forward to press a lingering kiss to the back of her neck. She smelled divine, a mix of the soap he'd used and perhaps the fragrance she'd worn this evening. Either way, he didn't care. He just wanted to breathe her in until he couldn't tell where she ended and he began. Still with his lips on her neck, he used his hands to rinse her skin thoroughly, lingering over her breasts again because he loved to hear the sounds she made as he touched her. And then he moved his hands lower, to the neat thatch of blond hair at the apex of her thighs.

She spread her legs as he edged closer and dropped her head on his shoulder as he swept his fingertips across her clit. The bath was warm but the heat coming from her core was hotter. Suddenly it wasn't enough to touch her with his hands. He wanted more. He tenderly eased her away from him and turned her to face him.

"I want you," he said, his voice thick with need. "All of you."

"I'm yours," she said simply.

"Then shall we take this to the bedroom?"

"I thought you'd never ask."

Fourteen

Jackson helped her step out of the bath and followed right behind her. Kristin couldn't resist letting her eyes rake over his body. He'd filled out some since the last time she'd seen him naked, and she certainly wasn't complaining. It was very definitely in all the right places.

Jackson grabbed two thick fluffy towels and, shaking one out, wrapped her in one and quickly used the other to wipe his body dry. Then, before she could do anything else, he swept her into his arms and walked through to the master bedroom. He put her carefully on the bed and unwrapped her as meticulously as a man with a long-anticipated gift.

Kristin's skin felt attuned to his every touch. As he stroked her face, her throat, her chest before tracing her nipples again, she concentrated on whatever part of her he touched.

"You always were exquisite," he said, bending to kiss her as he joined her on the bed and nestled his legs between hers.

His words were bittersweet, but she pushed aside the recriminations that continued to hover at the edge of her mind. She'd made her decision to accept his offer of friendship with benefits, and so far the benefits had been marvelous indeed. She looked forward to what came next. She didn't have to wait long. The hard evidence of his arousal lay hot and heavy at the juncture of her thighs and her whole body ached for his possession. She squirmed against him.

"Are you going to keep torturing me or are you going to get on with it?" she said, trying to inject a teasing note into her voice.

"This is torturing us both," he admitted, reaching for the bedside drawer next to her. "Best we get on with things, right? Then we can take our time after that."

She quivered with longing and anticipation as he sheathed himself and parted her thighs further so he fit perfectly right there. He held himself at the entrance to her body, and she could feel him tremble with restraint.

"Ready?" he growled.

"More than ready," she uttered, lifting her hips to him in supplication.

She felt him probing her and she clenched slightly around his tip before releasing him and feeling his entire length slide deep within her. She let her breath go on a sigh. This felt so right. So perfect. And when he began to move, she met his thrusts with perfect timing. Her body was so in sync with him it was as if the past had simply melted away and they were back to where they'd always been. Sublimely in tune with each other.

Kristin could feel her climax building. Bigger this time, deeper than before. She rode the waves, letting him take her to the ultimate completion and surrendering to the sensations that overtook her body. Pleasure made her throb and tingle from head to foot. Her arms wrapped tight around him and she shuddered as wave upon wave of satisfaction surged over her. And then she felt him come, too. His deep thrusts sent her body rippling into another, even more intense orgasm. She cried out with the force of it, her eyes closing and her body taut with the rush of fulfillment that swept through her.

Jackson collapsed against her, his breathing hard, his hands shaking as he took her face and kissed her deeply. She clenched on an aftershock and felt his body mirror her reaction.

He released her lips and rolled to one side, their bodies still joined, their skin slick with perspiration, their breathing still harsh and rapid. Words failed her. Sex with Jackson had always been incendiary, but this, this was something else entirely. And as she looked into his eyes, still clouded with the passion they'd shared, she knew with heart-stopping certainty that she'd never grown to hate him as she'd believed she had. In fact, the shattering truth was that she'd never stopped loving him, and acknowledging that terrified her beyond belief.

Jackson raised a hand and carefully pushed a lock of hair off her face.

"Stay right there."

He rose from the bed and went through to the bathroom. He returned in a moment, their flutes and the bottle of champagne in his hands.

"I think that deserves a toast, don't you?" he said as he climbed unselfconsciously onto the bed.

Kristin smiled and hauled herself up into a sitting position, holding her hand out for her glass. Jackson topped it off with more of the sparkling golden liquid. When he'd done the same with his own, he put the bottle on a bedside table and held his glass toward hers.

"To friendship," he said seriously.

Friendship? Kristin swallowed against the sudden knot that had appeared in her throat. What they'd just shared went well beyond friendship. But he'd set hard boundaries. He still mourned his wife, but he obviously mourned human contact and the intimacy of sex at the same time. No matter what it cost her, if she wanted to have at least this piece of him, she had to play by his rules. She raised her glass in a toast.

"To friendship," she repeated and drank deeply.

She'd indulged in pillow talk before but somehow it seemed inane to do that now. Especially when her world had shifted on its axis in the aftermath of their lovemaking. What had started as an idea to scratch an itch and potentially rid themselves of the burning urge to be together had transcended into so much more. To speak lightly of what had just happened between them would be to denigrate its seriousness, for her at least.

To her relief, Jackson seemed perfectly comfortable sitting in silence with her, taking an occasional sip from the wineglass he held in one hand while with the other he softly stroked the indentation of her hip. She felt dreadfully torn. This was the slow, secluded, private time of lovers, but her emotions threatened to choke her with their magnitude. Past hurts felt sharper, past losses deeper. To her shock and surprise, her eyes began to burn with unshed tears. She closed them briefly in an attempt to prevent their fall.

She felt Jackson take her glass from her hand.

"Are you okay?" he asked, concern deepening his voice.

"Just a little overwhelmed, to be honest."

"I know," he said. "Me, too."

She felt him shift on the bed and opened her eyes to see him pulling back the covers. She moved so she could do the same on her side.

"Come on," he said, holding out his arms for her. "Let's get some sleep and let it all sink in."

He turned off the lights, shifted to his side and she spooned against him in the dark. His arm curled around her waist, holding her firmly against him and for the first time in what felt like forever, she felt as if she was where she belonged. But she didn't belong there. This was only ever meant to be a temporary thing. Not a rekindling of what they'd had before. The tears she'd been holding in began to slowly spill down her cheeks, a mirror to the rain that fell steadily outside, echoing on the metal roof.

She could do this, she told herself, listening to Jack's breathing slow and deepen as he slid into sleep. She could do it because, even this, knowing it was purely a temporary arrangement, was better than nothing at all.

Her sleep was fitful and when, in the wee hours of the morning, she felt Jackson reach for her, she turned into his arms willingly. Anything to erase the turmoil of her mind, even if only for a while. They made love several times through the night. Long, slow and leisurely, and hard and fast as if their time together was short and ephemeral. And maybe it was because Kristin knew deep in her heart that she would not be able to sustain this for long. She'd recovered from losing Jackson once. She didn't think she'd manage to do it again.

When day broke, it was Christmas morning and she felt both energized by their lovemaking and shattered by her self-revelation at the same time. She gently pulled free of Jackson's hold, taking care not to wake him, and walked to the bathroom, where she picked up their clothing and placed it on the vanity before stepping into the shower. She turned on the faucet and stepped under the spray, closing her eyes and letting the water course over her.

She felt Jackson before she saw him. Felt his strength and hardness as he stepped into the shower behind her.

"Merry Christmas," he said, nuzzling against the sensitive spot just below her ear.

"Merry Christmas to you, too."

"Do you have to race away this morning?" he asked, reaching for the shower gel. After squirting some in his hands, he began to slick it over her body.

His strong hands moved firmly over her back and down to her buttocks before working their way around to her front, cupping her breasts and working her nipples into aching peaks before sliding over her ribs, past her waist and lower to where her body had already set up a demanding pulse. Her mind clouded, almost forgetting his question as she focused on his touch and what it did to her but she managed to gather her scrambled wits enough to nod.

"Brunch, at Logan and Honor's," she said in a voice that had turned husky with need.

After last night, she'd thought she'd feel totally sated, but it seemed that even after their lovemaking and the release it had brought her, over and over, she wanted more. No, she realized, she *needed* more. She needed Jackson—and on a scale that threatened to overwhelm her. She'd spent the past eleven years rebuilding herself from the ground up. She'd shored up her emotions, established her boundaries and erected the barriers that had allowed her to repair her shattered heart and tuck it away in a safe place. And with one night he'd effectively breached every safeguard she'd ever created. She was as open to him and to being hurt by him as she ever was. Could she trust him?

He'd made it clear he wanted no emotional entanglement. He'd likely withdraw from their arrangement if he knew the turmoil her heart and mind were in right now. Kristin made a decision then, one that she hoped would not come back to bite her. She'd roll with this for as long as she could. As pathetic as it made her in her own eyes, she'd take what he offered for as long as it was available. She'd healed her heart before; she could do it again. And she trusted that he would do his very best not to let her down.

She let her thoughts focus on the ministrations of his hands as he touched her, letting everything else fade into the background as his fingers gently parted the plump flesh between her thighs and touched her intimately. This was what she wanted. The oblivion he brought to her with his lovemaking. He stroked her clitoris in a tight circular motion and she felt the pressure of orgasm build within her. She put her hands on the shower wall in front of her, leaning forward and tilting her hips so her buttocks pressed against his groin.

"I have no protection in here," he said softly into her ear.

She shivered in delight as he increased the pressure of his fingers at the juncture of her thighs.

"I've been checked out. I'm clean and I'm on the Pill," she managed to say through clenched teeth.

"Me, too. I got checked before I asked you to sleep with me."

She bucked a little as zaps of sensation shot through to her very core.

"Then make love to me," she all but begged, pressing against him again.

She felt him adjust himself with his free hand, felt the swollen head of his penis at the entrance of her body. He hesitated, nearly killing her with anticipation, and then inch by slow inch he eased himself into her. It was all she needed to let go. On his first stroke deep inside her, it was as if he'd hit a switch and her body instantly went into a deep state of pulsating pleasure that built and built until her entire being rose high on another plane.

Jackson wrapped his arm around her, holding her tight to his body as his hips moved, his length sliding in and out, pushing her up, up, up on a scale of gratification that seemed to have no limit. Until, all at once, the sensation burst like a flower blooming, every sense unfurling and spreading until she shook all over and slumped against the wall, barely able to stand a moment longer. Jackson groaned against her neck, his own body rigid with the force of his climax, his legs trembling as they experienced an entirely new level of satisfaction together.

Water coursed over their bodies from the showerhead, sending tingles through her in aftershock. No one else had ever made her feel like this. Why did it have to be him?

She felt Jackson pull free and turned around to slip her arms around his waist and tuck herself against his chest. His heart pounded beneath her ear and his breathing was as rapid and fractured as her own. They held each other up like that for a long time. Lost in the wonder of what they'd just shared.

Eventually, though, it had to end, and she turned off the shower and pulled out of his arms.

"I must go," she said, simply.

He said nothing, just reached for a clean fluffy towel and handed it to her. They dried themselves in silence, and Kristin pulled on the clothes she'd worn the night before. When they were both dressed, they went downstairs and Kristin reached for the handbag she'd left near the entrance.

"I'll see you home," Jackson said as they both stood there looking at each other as if unsure what to say.

"I can call a ride," Kristin said, shaking her head.

"I said, I'll see you home," he said in a tone that brooked no argument.

Was he angry at her? At himself, maybe? Kristin couldn't tell, but he certainly didn't look happy.

"Fine. Thanks."

She felt uncomfortable as they headed to where he kept his car. The journey to her apartment continued in silence. Was this how things were to be going forward? She wasn't sure she could do this again if that was the case. Then she cast a look at him as he drove with concentrated attention on the road ahead and knew that if he so much as beckoned a finger she'd go running to him.

They pulled up outside her building and she started to get out the car, but Jackson put out a hand and stopped her.

"This wasn't how I imagined things," he said gruffly.

"What? The sex?" she asked bluntly.

"We both know that was way more than sex."

She slumped in her seat and studied his face. He

was a man in turmoil, she could see it in his eyes and the tight lines that now bracketed his mouth.

"It's okay, Jackson," she said carefully. "We both knew what we were getting into. We don't have to continue if you—"

"Oh, I want to, and that's more than half the problem."

"How so?" His answer intrigued her.

"Because I meant it when I said I'm not looking for emotional entanglement. I'm all out in that department. The tank is empty. I loved Annie and, being totally honest here, I don't believe I have it in me to love someone like that again. It wouldn't be fair to you not to make that utterly clear."

"I don't recall making any declarations in the last several hours, do you?" she said, unable to keep the bitterness out of her voice.

"I know, but Kristin, the sex, as you so succinctly put it, was so much more than that. I don't want to hurt you."

Again. The word, unsaid, hung in the air between them.

"You have no worries on that score. My heart is quite safe," Kristin lied. "Thanks for the ride and thanks for last night."

And then, gathering up her bag and all the dignity she had left, she got out of the car and walked into her building, fighting the nearly overwhelming urge to look back. It wouldn't change anything. It wouldn't soothe the pain that had settled in the vicinity of her heart. And, most importantly, it wouldn't change his mind.

Fifteen

Jack sat at his desk on Monday morning and stared at the paperwork marked High Priority, which had come through in his email. The DNA results submitted by the claimant in the Richmond family issue had been compared to the DNA taken from the Richmond children a year ago. There was a match, but, at the same time, there was another development that required him to speak with the family as soon as possible.

He called Kristin.

"Can you, Logan and Keaton meet with me at ten this morning? A meeting room in your office will be fine."

"Good morning to you, too," Kristin said crisply. "Why, yes, thank you, I had a lovely weekend. And you?"

Jackson closed his eyes and took a deep breath. "I'm sorry, yes, I did. Thank you for asking."

He'd spent several hours on Christmas Day with Ben, who'd been unusually out of sorts for the time of year. Normally he was bursting with exuberance on Christmas Day, but he'd been quieter than normal and prone to physical outbursts of frustration, and Jack had been forced to curtail his time with his stepson. They were the type of outbursts that had pushed Annie to put him into residential care in the first place, and were both a danger to him and potentially whoever was looking after him at the time. Worried about his stepson, Jack had thrown himself into work and yesterday had been spent reviewing client files while he tried to rid himself of the memory of slaking his lust on the one woman in the universe he should never have touched intimately ever again.

Making love to Kristin had been foolish in the extreme. Sure, being with her had felt right, not just physically, but on every other level, too. And he wanted to be more than just friends. He wanted to be the person who soothed her at the end of a tough day, the person who surprised her with breakfast in bed on the weekend. The person who helped make everything right with her world. But if he did that, wasn't he being disrespectful to Annie's memory? He didn't know who he'd been kidding when he'd thought he could revisit their passion without emotional attachment. Whether he'd wanted to or not, he'd been emotionally invested in each and every touch, and the memory of what they'd shared in the bathroom and between his sheets had haunted him from the moment she'd walked away from his car on Christmas morning.

She, quite clearly, had experienced no such issue. He didn't know if that was a relief or yet another frustration to add to the complication that had become his life. He drew in a deep breath and let it go slowly. He'd opt for relief. He didn't need complications, not with his responsibilities to Ben. Ben's carers had made it clear that he did not cope well with change and for Jackson to introduce a woman into Ben's life would create an overwhelming shift in his carefully constructed sphere. He knew he wasn't ready—and would likely never be able—to commit to another woman even if he wanted to. He wondered how long their friends-with-benefits arrangement could last.

"Look, I'm sorry I was abrupt," he continued. "I received some news this morning, and I want to inform you all at the same time."

"Relating to the claimant?" Kristin asked, all teasing gone from her voice.

"Yes. Are your brothers in the office?"

"They are. Hold on a moment while I message them. Ten, you said?"

"Yes," he affirmed.

He could hear her fingers flying over the keyboard of her computer and then two distinct pings as her brothers' answers obviously came back.

"We are confirmed. I'll book a meeting room now.

Do you want me to see if Fletcher, Mathias and Lisa can also attend?"

"Yes, it would be best but their attendance is not as critical."

"I'm intrigued, Jack. Is there anything you can tell me now?"

"It's to do with the DNA matching and it changes everything, in a good way. I'll call Hector and your mom."

"I believe they're busy finalizing everything for the wedding on Friday evening. I hope they can make it."

"It won't take up too much of their time."

They ended their call. Jackson called Hector, asking that he and Nancy join by video link with the others to save time. He caught a cab to the Richmond Tower and was surprised to see Kristin waiting for him at reception when he came out of the elevator.

"The others are already there," she said briskly. "Follow me."

Jackson looked at her as he walked closely behind. There hadn't been a single personal look or contact between them, and while that was exactly what he'd stipulated, he found he wasn't so keen on the idea in practice. Where was the warm, giving, loving woman he'd found solace with all through Friday night and Saturday morning? In her place was a sharp businesswoman with no time for pleasantries or even so much as a greeting.

He shook his head. He needed to let it go. This was what he'd wanted. No need to muddy the waters and complicate things now. Even so, as he walked behind her and studied the line of her back and the way her dress fitted her body so perfectly, he couldn't help feeling a sexual tug. He was so captured by his feelings he didn't notice she'd stopped at a door. He almost barreled straight into her. She gave him a quizzical look.

"Everything okay, Jack?" she asked with one eyebrow quirked.

"Fine. Everything's fine. Let's get this show on the road."

He entered the meeting room and greeted the family members assembled there. On the big screen he spied Nancy and Hector along with Lisa and Mathias. Fletcher, it transpired, was away on a short break in the Blue Ridge Mountains. A part of Jack envied the man his respite from the complications of business and everyday living.

"Thank you for agreeing to meet at such short notice," he said to everyone.

"We're intrigued by the urgency. Is there any new information about the person claiming to be our new sibling? I assume this has to do with the deadline getting closer," Mathias said onscreen.

"It does, and in particular with the DNA report they submitted and the comparison to the information held from the time Logan returned to the family. We managed to expedite the results, and—" Jackson took in a deep breath and looked at each family member in turn before letting his gaze settle on Kristin. "There's a match."

The room went completely silent, then erupted in a series of questions and expressions of anger. Nancy had gone completely white.

Jackson asked for silence. "If you could let me continue. There is a match but it's not the kind of match you would expect between siblings."

"Jackson, please, stop beating around the bush," Logan said. "We need a straight answer. What kind of match is it?"

"Well, it's a one hundred percent match to one of you—Kristin, in fact."

All eyes turned to Kristin, who looked shocked.

"Hey," she said, putting her hands up in a gesture of surrender. "I didn't instigate this, I promise. I have more than my fair share, and I certainly am not after anything more."

Keaton turned his gaze to Jackson. "So the claim is fraudulent?"

"I believe so. Somehow, someone has accessed material with Kristin's DNA. We've appealed to the lab that supplied the claimant's report for exactly what material was used to extract the DNA information. They're not under obligation to tell us but I did suggest that the police will become involved in this matter shortly and that if they could cooperate with us that would be beneficial." On cue, his phone pinged on the table in front of him. "Ah, let me check, that may be what we're waiting for."

Jackson lifted his phone and scanned the incoming message. The contents surprised him. He looked up.

"Well?" Keaton demanded. "Is it the information you were waiting for?"

"Yes, it is. Apparently the material supplied by the claimant was, oddly, leg hair."

"Leg hair?" Nancy said in shock. "But how?"

Kristin's brow was furrowed but cleared as something obviously came to her mind.

"What is it, Kristin?" Jackson asked.

"The cosmetologist who does my legs at my regular day spa is new and was asking all sorts of questions about me at my last visit when I went for waxing. She seemed to know a lot already, but no more than what made the papers when Logan came back to us last year. Do you think it might be her?"

"I'll get our investigator to look into it straight away. Do you have her details?"

"Yes, I have her card in my handbag in my office. Do you want me to go and get it?"

"In a moment, I can come with you. Now, does anyone else have any other questions?"

Nancy cleared her throat. "So, she definitely isn't one of Douglas's children?"

"It is certainly looking that way," Jackson said.

"What will become of her?"

"If we can establish she is behind the claim and the implied blackmail, we will hand the matter over to the police together with all our findings and correspondence."

"So that's that? The matter is over?" Nancy pressed.

"Yes, I believe so. For you as a family, at least.

For the person involved, their troubles are just beginning."

The older woman sighed and looked at Hector in relief. "I was so scared," she said. "It was hard enough learning about Eleanor, but others? It makes a woman begin to doubt her own sanity."

"There's nothing wrong with your sanity, my dear," Hector hastened to assure her. "The only person whose sanity is in question is Douglas's and he's no longer here to defend his behavior."

"Well, it looks as if we can relax now," Nancy said with a grin that showed just how much lighter she felt in spirit now that the threat of more bad publicity had been averted. "And you will all be at the rehearsal dinner on Thursday, right?"

Everyone gave their assent and closed their video links or filed out of the room, with the exception of Kristin, who shut the door behind Logan as he left, and turned to face Jackson. Before he could say anything, she crossed the distance between them, took his face in hers and kissed him thoroughly before letting him go just as abruptly.

Desire instantly flared inside him and despite everything he'd told himself to do with remaining emotionally distant, there was a part of him that had craved exactly this from Kristin. A part of him that wanted more and that urged him to take a risk on letting love grow between them again. Who are you kidding, that pesky voice said insolently at the back of his mind. You know you want to. Just do it. He clamped down on the thought before he did something stupid, like grab Kristin in his arms and tell her how he really felt.

"I needed that," she said. "Spending most of the weekend with my family has left me desperate for some benefits. How about my place, tonight? I can even serve you dinner if you like."

Jackson forced his lips into a smile. "You've learned to cook?"

"I can reheat a dinner as well as the next person. Seriously, though, there's a Vietnamese place nearby that delivers, and they do the most delicious food. Shall we say seven?"

"Sure, works for me."

She chewed her lip a moment, as if she were debating what she would say next.

"Thanks for what you've done for us, Jack. We all really appreciate it. You dealt with this entire issue very professionally, and you've saved us from a great deal of trouble and angst. Especially Mom."

"Only doing my job," he said, but he couldn't help feeling a kernel of pride flicker to life at her praise. "It was important to me to prove to you that you could trust me, Kristin. I know you had valid reasons for doubting me and whether I'd be a good fit professionally for your family. I hope I've managed to allay those concerns."

She looked at him in complete silence for several seconds. Had he gone too far saying what he had? Would she forever remain suspicious of his reliability?

"Jack, just to make it clear. I wouldn't have slept with you again if I didn't trust you."

He inclined his head in acknowledgement, the sense of relief that swamped him almost robbing him of speech. He shouldn't feel this way, he told himself. It shouldn't be this important to him, but it was, and hearing the words from her mouth gave him a sense of well-being he hadn't realized he'd been missing for a very long time.

Kristin opened the door.

"I'd better get back to work. I've got a lot to get through before taking Mom for her final fitting. Which reminds me, have you been fitted for your suit for the wedding?"

"I have. I pick it up on Thursday."

"Good, I'd hate anything to mar Mom and Hector's special day."

"I hear you've done an incredible job helping your mom pull it all together so quickly."

"I love her. I'd do anything for her to make sure she's happy. She's had a really hard time this past year, losing Dad and then discovering what a piece of work he was. This latest business took a toll on her. She may not have shown it to everyone, but I know it rocked her. She deserves so much better than that."

"You all do."

Her lips tweaked into a half smile. "Thanks. See you tonight, then. I'll leave your name with the concierge, so you'll be able to come straight up to my apartment."

Jackson watched as she left the room and wondered at the wisdom of availing himself of the benefits she promised so soon after their last entanglement. It could get to be a habit. It could lead to more complications. While she'd been matter-of-fact about the request to join her tonight, he hadn't been oblivious to the anticipation that had shone in her eyes. Did it mean she was hoping for more than he was prepared to offer? And, even more importantly, was he ready to offer more now, too?

Sixteen

It was New Year's Eve. Kristin checked the floral displays one last time before returning upstairs to her mom's bedroom to finish getting ready for the wedding. Guests had begun to arrive and take their seats in the ballroom that overlooked the water. She'd thought Nancy would be a bundle of nerves tonight, but instead she was a picture of joy and serenity.

"Mom," she said as she rejoined her mother. "I can't believe how calm you are about all this."

"What's to be nervous about? I'm marrying a man who thinks the sun rises and sets with me. A man whom I love more than life itself. I'm thrilled we're embarking on a new life together. We've both known much joy and sorrow over the years, and we know that we can deal with anything together."

Kristin felt tears spring to her eyes at her mom's heartfelt words. She wished that for herself, too, with her whole heart. So as not to alert her mom to her near overwhelming emotional reaction, she turned to her extract Nancy's cream silk gown with its gold lace overlay and matching long-line gold jacket from its garment bag.

From the moment she'd seen Nancy in the set, she'd known it was perfect for her. It was a far cry from the neat navy blue suit her mom had worn for her registry office marriage to Douglas Richmond all those years ago. Kristin also took the shoebox from the wardrobe that held the matching gold pumps her mom would wear tonight.

"Come on, let's get you ready for your groom. I bet he can't wait to see you," Kristin said with a level of bonhomie she didn't quite feel.

"Sweetheart, you don't have to try so hard," Nancy said, putting a hand on her daughter's arm. "Your time will come. I know it."

"I'm not trying hard, Mom. I am truly happy for you and Hector." Darn, she'd failed to keep her feelings from her mom, but then again, if anyone in this world knew her well enough to know when she was faking, it was Nancy.

"I'm glad you are, my darling girl. I'm sorry things haven't worked out for you the way you would have wanted, though."

"My life is just as it needs to be. Don't worry about me, okay? Today is your day. Yours and Hector's," Kristin hastened to reassure her.

"I'm your mother. I'm always going to worry about you," Nancy said with a laugh. She leaned forward and kissed Kristin lightly on the cheek. "But you're right. We need to finish getting ready. It's almost time."

Kristin helped her mother dress in the beautifully finished dress and jacket and then slipped into the simpler, pale coffee-colored cocktail dress with its bolero style jacket, which she'd chosen to wear as her mom's attendant. Together they stood in front of the mirror and admired each other's appearance.

"We look great, Mom. But you, you are totally going to knock Hector's socks off when he sees you."

"And the rest of his clothes, too, I hope," Nancy said with a giggle.

"Mom!" Kristin protested but then joined her mom in laughter.

This was what life should be like, she thought as she reached for her mom's bouquet. Nancy had chosen creamy roses accented with wildflowers and berries in burnished bronze tones, while Kristin's bouquet was a deeper shade of the burnished accents. Together, they descended the stairs and walked toward the ballroom where the ceremony was about to take place.

Kristin reached for her mom's hand and gave it a squeeze as they approached the ballroom's double doors, manned by Martha.

"You both look so beautiful," the housekeeper said, brushing a tear from her cheek. "May tonight bring you the happiness you deserve."

"Thank you, Martha. I couldn't have made it through this year without you propping me up."

"It was my honor," she said. "Are you both ready?"

Nancy and Kristin nodded, and Martha opened the doors. The music inside the ballroom changed to the traditional wedding march. Kristin began to walk down toward where Hector and the celebrant waited. Hector, the celebrant and Keaton, she realized. *Keaton?* Where was Jackson? He'd been at the rehearsal dinner last night, and he'd appeared as hale and hearty as ever, even if there'd been a slight air of distraction about him.

A sick feeling settled in the pit of Kristin's stomach. If he'd been hurt or taken ill, she knew she would have heard about it before tonight. There was no reason for Jackson not to be here today for what was one of the most important events in her family's year. He was supposed to be supporting Hector. Instead, he was nowhere to be seen. A darkening sense of déjà vu began to fill her, but she kept her smile painted on her face and forced herself to keep walking slowly to the men in the front. Around her, she heard a collective gasp of admiration as her mom began to follow her down the aisle, and she saw Hector's face glow with so much love and pride as Nancy approached that Kristin felt tears burn her eyes again.

She stood to the side and watched her mom stand beside the man she clearly loved with all her heart. Her gaze flicked to the assembled group of family and friends. Tami sat with Honor and Logan, each of them with their attention concentrated on Nancy.

Even her half siblings from Virginia were here, along with a few of her mom and Hector's closest friends. But no sign of Jackson.

She'd told him last night how much she was looking forward to seeing him today. Couldn't he at least have texted her? Ice began to form around her heart. She'd been a fool. A complete and utter fool to have let her guard down. To think that he could be relied upon. To believe or even begin to hope that he was different. But no, he hadn't changed at all. He was every bit as unreliable and cavalier with her feelings as he'd been eleven years ago. She should have known better than to trust him, ever. And she'd be damned if she'd go running after him as she'd tried to last time.

As she turned to face the celebrant and stand by her mom, she made herself a promise. She would never let herself feel another thing for him. In fact, she doubted she'd be able to trust herself to feel anything for anyone, ever again. She'd been so stupid to think that perhaps their temporary arrangement of friendship with benefits could evolve into something more. Something stronger and more mature than their first love for each other. Something that might even last and stand the test of time. But they'd been pipe dreams. The stuff of fairy tales.

He'd warned her that he could give her no more than just sex. She'd agreed to that and thought she was strong enough to accept that was all they'd ever have. But her stupid heart had let her down. What the hell was wrong with her that she couldn't see the writing on the wall when it was written in letters six feet high? Why was she so thoroughly destined to fail in her relationships?

As the celebrant intoned the words that would bind her mom and Hector together, and she heard them pledge their love to each other, Kristin made herself a promise. This, love, wasn't for her. Even hope was too much for her. From now on she would encase her heart in the thickest wall of concrete and shore it up with razor wire for good measure. Work would be her panacea and thank goodness she had enough of that to carry her through.

She'd take joy in her brother's relationships with their partners and the new generation that was coming. She'd celebrate the fact her mom had found love again and would never have to be alone. But she'd expect none of that for herself. She couldn't. It simply hurt too much.

The night continued in a vein of joyful celebration with a dinner and speeches and the cutting of a two-tier cake. Through it all, Kristin kept a smile pasted on her face. No one would ever know the pain she bore right now. No one would even suspect she'd felt her world crumble to dust when her every last fear around Jackson Jones had come to pass. Jackson had chosen not to be here and chosen not to tell her why, just like he'd chosen to walk out on his promises to her the first time. It ended here.

She danced with Hector after the meal.

"Thank you for being Nancy's support today,"

Hector said warmly as they took their turn around the ballroom floor.

"It was my honor," Kristin said softly. "I thought Jackson was meant to be your support person today. Did something happen to him?"

"A family matter," Hector said briefly.

Kristin almost missed a step. She knew Jackson had no family. Had he lied to a man who was supposed to be one of his best friends? Or had he lied to her instead? How could she have been so stupid as to trust him? One of her brothers cut in at that moment, preventing her from pressing for more information, but it made no difference. Jackson wasn't here when he had said he would be.

She forced herself to look happy through the rest of the celebrations and, at midnight, when the fireworks went off over the lake, she gathered with everyone else and oohed and aahed in appreciation. By the time Hector and Nancy headed off to their honeymoon hotel, their car festooned with ribbons and even a set of tin cans tied to the rear fender, she felt her smile beginning to slip.

The evening was over. With Martha, she saw the guests off home and supervised the cleaning crew as they tidied the house back to its usual elegant perfection. Her feet were aching when the ride she'd booked arrived to take her home again. Through it all, she held herself together. Through the drive home, the ride in the elevator to her floor, getting into her apartment and disrobing from the beautiful outfit she'd worn tonight. The outfit she'd so looked forward to having Jackson see her in. She kicked it to the corner of her bedroom. She doubted she'd ever wear it again, no matter how joyful the occasion it was associated with.

She took a quick shower and, once dry, pulled on an oversize T-shirt she liked to sleep in and walked to her bedroom window, staring out at the dark night.

It was a new year.

A new start.

She'd never felt so alone.

Over the weekend that rang in the start of the New Year, Kristin kept herself busy by going into the office. It certainly beat being alone with her thoughts. She'd been invited to dinner with Keaton and Tami on Sunday night and had initially thought to refuse. But Tami had begged her to come so they could start planning their wedding. She wanted Kristin to be her maid of honor.

"Always a bridesmaid," Kristin muttered as she backed up her files and shut down her computer.

She flicked a glance at her phone, which she'd kept on a silent setting so she could work uninterrupted, and was surprised to see she'd missed two calls from Jackson. Plus, there was both a voice and a text message from him. She had no desire to hear or read his excuses and deleted both unheard and unread—in fact she deleted their entire message thread for good measure before heading down to the parking garage. On the way to Keaton and Tami's apartment, she swung by a liquor store to buy a bottle of wine and made it to their place in good time. When she'd found a parking spot and slung her bag over her shoulder she felt her phone vibrate again.

Thinking it might be her mom calling to let her know they'd arrived in Hawaii for their honeymoon, she quickly glanced at the screen. It was Jackson calling again. Kristin rejected the call and threw her phone back in her bag, wondering if she ought to block his number.

She knew she'd have to face up to him at some stage; after all he was their family attorney. But no one said she had to continue to socialize with him outside of his duty to her family.

Duty. She shook her head. He hadn't even managed the one thing that Hector had asked him to do. It made her mad, just thinking about it. So mad, in fact, that she set the bottle of wine she'd been carrying on the sidewalk between her feet and dug her phone out of her bag. She opened a new message and addressed it to Jackson.

Stop messaging me and trying to call. I no longer wish to maintain our arrangement. I no longer wish to see you or speak to you outside of your responsibilities to my family. Is that clear?

She waited a minute for his reply. Nothing came through. Typical, she thought. He wanted her to be available to him when it suited him but couldn't even respond when she texted him. That was just fine by her. She put her phone in her bag, picked up the wine and finished walking the short distance to Keaton's apartment building. She'd have a fun night tonight. She'd help Tami start the wedding planning, and she'd even show enthusiasm for the event.

But as far as Jackson Jones was concerned—actually, as far as any man was concerned—her heart was now firmly encased in impenetrable layers. She did not plan to allow the barrier to be lifted for anyone ever again. It hurt too much, and she'd had enough of that to last a lifetime.

The evening with Keaton and Tami turned out to be enjoyable. By the time Kristin arrived home, she felt mellow and relaxed. Despite herself, she checked her phone again. Nothing from Jack. Well, maybe he'd taken her literally and hadn't seen the need to respond. He certainly hadn't seen the need to inform her that he wouldn't be there at the wedding last Friday, so clearly he remained on trend in that department.

Monday morning rolled around all too quickly. Kristin was in the office when she received an email notification from Jackson's office. Not from Jackson himself, she noted, but from his assistant. It was addressed to all the family and the header stated, "CLAIMANT EXPOSED." She avidly read the email, which informed the Richmonds that the cosmetologist who had done Kristin's waxing was one of two daughters of Jenna Emerson. The other daughter, surprisingly enough, was a reporter and, Kristin suspected, the newswoman who'd questioned her before the charity gala.

Everything was falling neatly into place. The girls had apparently hatched the idea together while going through their late mother's things. While neither of them was a child of Douglas Richmond, their mother's diaries had detailed a torrid affair she and Douglas had had before she'd been paid off and asked to leave Richmond Developments. The matter was now in the hands of the police, who would be speaking to the women regarding blackmail and extortion charges.

Kristin sank in her seat, hardly daring to believe this latest drama was over. Without Jackson's dogged determination to overturn every rock and follow every potential lead, who knew where they'd have been right now?

There was a knock at her office door, and Logan opened it on her command and entered.

"Did you get the news?" he asked as he took the seat opposite her.

"I did. It's a relief, right?"

"It sure is. Not that another sibling would be unwelcome, but one would hope that if there are any more they would come to us openly."

"Do you think there are more? By the looks of things, Dad was very, um, active in that department."

Logan shrugged. "Who knows? I guess we have to be prepared for anything."

"Well, I'm glad we can move forward again without worrying about this hanging over our heads. How's Honor feeling?"

"Still a bit queasy in the mornings, but she's handling it well."

"And you? Looking forward to the new arrival?" she asked with a tiny bit of envy.

A huge smile spread across Logan's face. "Yeah, I am. We both are. We're already busy choosing potential names and thinking about decorating a nursery. First step, though, is to buy a house. I want my kid to grow up feeling grass beneath its feet in the summer. We were thinking of looking for something closer to Mom's since she and Hector have decided to remain at her place."

Kristin smiled as Logan filled her in on their plans, and the kernel of envy that had formed before was now a hard knot in her stomach. Her choice, she reminded herself. If she wasn't prepared to put her heart on the line again, then she'd have to come to terms with that green-eyed monster and learn to tuck it away where it wouldn't color other people's joy with its unpleasantness. Kristin snapped back to attention when she realized Logan had asked her a question.

"I'm sorry, I drifted away there for a minute," she apologized. "What did you ask?"

"I asked you how you are. Really are, not just the surface answer I know you're about to give me. Honor and I are worried about you."

"About me? Whatever for?" she asked, avoiding answering the question.

"Mom told us you and Jackson had a past. And it was clear to anyone with eyes in their face that there were still sparks between you. I thought you two were getting along but then he didn't come to the wedding. Now you're looking like you did before he reappeared in your life. What's going on, Kristin?"

"Nothing's going on."

And it's none of your business, she wanted to add. But he was her brother, and despite the fact he'd only been in her life for a little over a year now, he took his responsibilities to his family seriously.

Logan stared at her, a frown of concern pulling between his eyebrows.

"You can talk to me, y'know. A problem shared is a problem halved and all that."

She forced herself to smile. "Thanks, I appreciate it. But I'm not ready to talk about it just yet. In fact, I may not be ready to talk about it any time."

"I'm here if you need me. We all are." He sighed before continuing. "Have you talked to Jackson yet?"

"No, and I don't see the need to. Whatever we had is over. This time for good."

"I'm sorry to hear that. You deserve to be happy, Kristin. I thought, on Christmas Eve, that maybe you and Jackson had resolved the differences that had been so apparent when we met him at the beginning of the month."

She'd thought so, too, but apparently not. A woman could be taken for a fool only so many times before she read the writing that was starkly painted on the wall.

"We worked through that. It won't affect his dealings with our family. And I think he's proven his capability in that regard."

"So, there's nothing more between you than a business relationship."

Kristin felt a sharp twist deep in her chest. "Absolutely nothing," she said firmly.

"Damn, I'm sorry to hear that."

"Don't worry. I'm a big girl. I can cope. And, for the record, what is it with all you happy couples that you can't stand to see a singleton without wanting them matched up with someone else?"

She forced herself to keep her tone light, and it had the desired effect. Logan laughed as he rose to leave.

"Point taken," he said, turning for the door.

"Logan?" Kristin called out.

He stopped in his tracks and faced her.

"Thanks. I do mean that. And I'm glad you've got my back if I need you."

He gave her a smile and a nod and left her office. She sat there a while longer before picking up her phone. Her finger hovered over Jackson's number before she put the phone down again. No, it was better this way.

A clean cut with no regrets. Well, perhaps not an entirely clean cut, given they would still have to work together on the family's legal matters, but as far as her personal life was concerned, he was out. It was the right thing to do.

But if it was the right thing, why did she feel so utterly desolate and unhappy?

Seventeen

Jackson pulled his car up in the visitor parking outside Kristin's apartment building and turned off the ignition. For a full five minutes he sat there, carefully considering what he had to say. She hadn't taken his calls. She'd ignored his messages and her text had been clear and concise. She had excised him from her private life with meticulous precision.

It had been a week since he'd been forced to let her family down at the wedding. A hellish week that had seen him emotionally dragged through the wringer and back out again. Ben's cardiac arrest had taken them all by surprise, and Jack had tried to do his best for his stepson. Staying by his side day and night at the hospital as Ben's condition deteriorated farther and farther. Being strong for Ben's grandparents as they visited each day. Eventually, the doctors had told them that the oxygen starvation he'd suffered immediately after the arrest had left Ben with such severe brain damage that there was no reasonable hope of recovery.

He'd fought the doctors for days. Begged them to keep Ben on the ventilator that was keeping him breathing and giving him a chance. But then this afternoon, Ben's heart had given out completely, and his all too short life had ended. Jack wasn't sure about his beliefs about the hereafter but he liked to think that at least Ben was with Annie now, although that was little consolation for his loss.

Before the wedding, he'd only contacted Hector to explain, asking him to keep it in his confidence. In the days that followed he'd realized he needed to talk with someone—specifically with Kristin. But his texts and calls had gone unread and unanswered, leaving him further adrift. He hated the sensation. It reminded him too much of how he'd felt when Annie had passed away and made him begin to understand just how Kristin must have felt when he disappeared on her. But the key thing was, he needed her, and he'd only just begun to understand and accept that. But how was he going to get past her barriers now?

He looked up at Kristin's building, to her floor and the windows that faced the street. Lights glowed from inside. Would she agree to see him? He'd never know if he didn't get out of the car and go and find out. And somehow he had to explain why he'd let her down again.

He forced himself to alight from the car, grief and exhaustion dragging at every cell in his body. He still had so much to attend to. Appointing a funeral director, arranging notices, clearing Ben's room at the residential unit where he'd been cared for, choosing the outfit for Ben to wear—the list went on. But right now he needed someone, and Kristin was the only person he wanted. The past few days had shown him that he needed her now like he'd never needed her before.

It had been a hard road to admit that he still loved her. Harder yet to accept that he always had. He'd believed he'd been able to shut off that part of himself. That he couldn't have loved Annie the way he had, or had the life with her that they'd shared, if he'd still loved another woman. But he'd been so very wrong.

Each woman had been individual in her own right. His love for each was individual, too. He'd made himself walk away from Kristin before, thinking that if he made a clean break that it would be easier, somehow. But he'd been more wrong than he'd ever allowed himself to admit. It hadn't been easy. Not on him and certainly not on her. Somehow he had to make amends and it started with the truth and admitting his feelings. Maybe today wasn't the best day, given the week he'd had, but if not now, then when?

He gave his name to the attendant on the front desk and the man waved him through. Obviously, Kristin hadn't had him removed from the approved visitors list yet. Or maybe, despite what she'd said to him via text message, she wanted him to fight for the tenuous relationship they'd created. He hoped the latter was true.

Friends with benefits? How stupid was that? There was nothing friendly in what they'd shared. Every touch, every kiss had been given from the depths of his heart and soul. Accepting that as his truth had been the challenge. And now he had to make her see it, too.

He exited the elevator on her floor and walked to her apartment entrance and pressed the buzzer. It wasn't long before he heard her at the door. There was a hesitation, as if she'd seen him through the peephole and was debating whether or not to let him in.

He injected his voice with a surety he was far from feeling. "Kristin? Please. I'll wait here as long as it takes, but I really need to see you, to talk."

Still she waited on the other side. Then, thankfully, he heard her disengage the locks and pull the door open.

"You look like hell," she said, her eyes raking over him.

There was no welcome in her gaze, no heat in her eyes, nor anticipation in her expression. Not even as much as a tiny smile graced her beautiful face. It was as if she'd locked up her emotions and thrown away the key. And it hurt to know he was the one responsible for doing that to her.

"Thanks. May I come in?"

"I opened the door, didn't I?"

She stepped aside and he entered her foyer and

waited for her to close the door. The subtle waft of her fragrance teased his nostrils and he wanted, more than anything, to take her in his arms and bury his face in her neck. To inhale the essential scent that was her and to let go of the fiercely held reins on his grief.

"Come in and sit before you fall down," she said bluntly. "Have you eaten?"

He couldn't remember the last time he'd eaten or what it had been. Probably something Ben's grandmother had brought up from the hospital cafeteria. He followed Kristin into the sitting room and sat on the couch.

"I'm okay."

"I didn't ask if you're okay, I asked if you'd eaten."

"Not in a while, no."

Jack lifted a hand and rubbed his jaw. His fingers scraped on the bristles there, reminding him he hadn't shaved for several days now, either. He must look a wreck.

"I'll get you a sandwich." As he started to protest she raised a hand. "It's no bother. You really look like you need it."

"As long as you don't lace it with strychnine," he said with a poor attempt at humor.

"Don't tempt me," she answered, her tone as flat as her expression.

He watched her as she went to her kitchen and quickly put together something for him. She was back in minutes and handed him a plate, together with a can of cola.

"Eat. Drink. Then you can talk."

He didn't argue. He hadn't even realized he was hungry until he saw the fresh sourdough bread sandwich made with pickles, cheese and a generous slab of bologna. His mouth watered as he took the first bite. The sandwich was gone in no time, and the cola, too. He wiped his face with the paper napkin she'd provided and put it on the empty plate on the table in front of him.

"More?" she asked, rising from her seat.

He reached out and grabbed her hand. "No, please. Sit. I need to get some things off my chest. I'd be grateful if you could let me say my piece. I promise I'll leave when I'm done."

"Go on, then. Talk."

Jackson drew in a deep breath and let it go slowly. "I guess I'd better start at the beginning."

"Usually works best," Kristin said cynically.

He looked at her carefully. There was tension in every line of her body and she still wore a visage of indifference. Somehow he needed to break through that line of defense she'd erected. He only hoped the truth would be enough.

"The reason I didn't make it to the wedding was because my stepson, Ben, suffered a cardiac arrest."

Kristin gasped softly in response. "You never told me you had a son. Did Hector know about him? "

Jackson nodded and saw the pain that lashed her as it sunk in that he'd kept something so vital from her. He wished he could have turned back the clock and done things differently but he knew, only too well, that was an impossible feat. And by doing what he'd done all those years ago the first time he'd left her, he'd merely compounded the damage by keeping things to himself again.

"I'm sorry I never told you about him. After all the publicity surrounding her affair with Ben's father, Annie was very protective of him and their privacy. I guess I was so used to observing her wishes on that score it became second nature not to talk about him. He was a special man. He died this morning."

She made a sound that was a cross between shock and sympathy. Then her brows furrowed. "A special man? He wasn't a kid?"

"Annie was much older than me when we met. Ben was her son. He was only a few years younger than me and, due to complications during his delivery, he was born with intellectual difficulties that made him challenging as he grew older and stronger. He was prone to rages and, on a few occasions, hurt her quite badly. Unintentionally, of course, but she knew she couldn't care for him on her own any longer. At first, she was reluctant to start a relationship with me at all. I was too young, she told me, and she didn't think I would cope with being left one day with an adult special needs son. But I proved to her that we could be great together. We went out a few times and, eventually, she introduced me to Ben. He doesn't take to strangers and I knew it would be a deal breaker if he didn't warm to me but luckily Ben liked me, too.

"Annie finally saw that she could have more than

what she'd allowed herself. She could have a relationship and still be a great mom to Ben. He was in a residential care facility by then, and it made her feel so terribly guilty at first, but his behavior began to improve little by little. She would have him on weekends when we could give him our fullest attention. Occasionally she'd bring him up here to Seattle to visit with his grandparents. She was originally from Seattle, and her parents are nearby."

"That must have been hard. Having to win her trust and that of her son, too," Kristin said.

He felt himself relax a little. She sounded as if she was thawing just a little.

"It was hard but it was worth every second. When Annie was diagnosed with cancer she went down really fast. I sometimes wonder if she hadn't been with me, she might have sought medical help sooner, but it is what it is. We can't turn back the clock."

"Why would you say that? Why wouldn't she have gone to the doctor earlier if she knew something was wrong?"

"Because she devoted all of her care and time and attention between me and Ben, and her clients, of course. She left no room for herself. She ignored all the warning signs until it was too late for effective treatment."

"You can't blame yourself for that, Jackson."

"I know, but I still feel responsible, you know?"

"Yeah, probably in much the same way that I know Honor still feels some responsibility for my father's fatal brain bleed when he died. They were arguing. It made no difference because he was a ticking time bomb as far as vascular issues went and he'd ignored his health for too long, but I can imagine that what you're going through is very similar to her situation then."

"Thanks. When we knew she wasn't going to get better, I did everything I could to make sure her final months were as happy as they could be. We had Ben to the house as often as we could, but he didn't cope well with her diminishing health. She found that hard, we all did. Ben and I became a lot closer then, and when Annie died I devoted as much time as I could to him. It helped me grieve her loss. And then Hector contacted me with his offer.

"Turned out, on Annie's instructions, he'd also found the perfect residential unit for Ben here in Seattle—a place close enough that her parents—his grandparents—could visit weekly. Hector and Annie had been in discussions for some time, and she had already conducted video interviews with the staff and management and had a virtual tour of the facility. It felt as if, even in death, she was looking out for us. It was the kind of woman she was."

"She sounds incredible," Kristin murmured.

"She was. On her deathbed I promised her I would always look after Ben. While we're not too dissimilar in age, he was like a six-year-old boy inside. He needed a parental figure and I was it. As he's grown older he hasn't coped with change as well. The move to Seattle almost crushed him, but he was starting to like his new care facility more and more. He loved coming to spend an evening with me on the weekends.

"Kristin, I want you to know that I take my responsibilities seriously. After that first time, when I left you in college, I learned a valuable lesson about people and life in general. I never reached out to you because I knew I'd hurt you and didn't want to reignite that pain for you when you might have already moved on. This time around, being together the way we've been, it's taught me another valuable lesson. One I tried to ignore at first but which I can't overlook. I still love you. I always have. You were and always will be my first love."

"I'm sorry, Jackson, but I find that hard to believe. People who love don't let each other down. Especially not when it's really important. They don't keep important truths from each other."

There was a bitterness to her voice that struck him to his core.

"I know, and I should have called you last Friday. But when I got the call that Ben had had a major heart event, my first thought was for him. I called Hector quickly on the way to the hospital and asked him not to explain my absence because it wasn't something I wanted you to find out through someone else. I had realized that I needed to tell you about Ben, but his heart attack came out of the blue. I didn't leave his side until he died this afternoon."

Grief swelled from deep inside and threatened to choke him with its sheer volume. Silence stretched between the two of them.

"I guess you're wondering where that leaves us," he said heavily.

This was going to be the hard part. Convincing Kristin that his feelings for her were real. That they'd never left him.

"There isn't an us, Jackson. I thought I could do the friends-with-benefits thing, but I can't. Trust is a major issue for me. Not just after what happened when we were younger but with a more recent relationship and with my Dad as well. I'm sorry about your stepson. I truly am. But it doesn't change anything for me. You chose not to tell me about your parents until recently and then only because you could have been on the verge of losing my family's business. You also chose not to tell me about your late wife until provoked, or your stepson or why you couldn't be there at Hector and Mom's wedding.

"I had begun to believe that you were different to what you were before. That maybe, with time, we'd be able to work beyond our past and create a future together. That you'd learned how essential good communication is between two people who have feelings for one another." She shook her head sadly. "But it's not going to happen. I'm confident you are the best lawyer for our family. You have more than proved yourself on that issue. But you can't seem to communicate with me unless it's with your body and that's not enough. I need more than that. Look, let me explain. After Dad died I was crushed. We'd loved and trusted him our whole lives and he'd cheated on us all. Then, when the corporate espionage was exposed, I learned that my right-hand man in the office—a man I thought I'd started to fall in love with and maybe had a future with and whom I'd welcomed into my bed—was using me to pass on information to our main competitor. Discovering that abuse of my trust nearly destroyed me. So understand this, if nothing else, I won't let you hurt me again."

Jackson listened to her with a heart that grew heavier with each word she uttered. He'd messed up. Totally and utterly. There was no returning from this unless she had a change of heart, and it would be unkind to try and force her to do that.

"I never wanted to hurt you, ever. I love you, Kristin. Your happiness means more to me now than I ever understood when I was younger. Hardship has taught me a lot of things, and among them, when to walk away. I thought I was doing the right thing when I walked away from you in college. I learned a long time ago that it wasn't. But please understand that as I walk away from you now, it's because you want me to and for no other reason. I want what is best for you, always. All I ask is that you let yourself be happy, Kristin."

"You think I don't want to be happy?"

"Oh, I know you do. But the hurt I caused you, along with the things life has thrown at you, have made you shore up your defenses. I think you'd rather be alone than take a risk on someone."

"I took a risk on our friends-with-benefits thing," she said defensively.

"A risk? Or was it an easy out like I thought it was for me? The fun without the commitment? I have to be honest with you, Kristin. I can no more see you as a friend now than I could the first time I met you. There is something about you that completes me and to which I'm drawn like a magnet. When we're together, it's like we're two halves of the same soul. And when we're apart, I'm only half me. But I can live with that, if that's what you want, *because* it's what you want. Even if it isn't what we both need."

He rose from the couch and shoved his hands in his pockets, knowing that if he didn't he'd do something dumb like reach for her, pull her into his arms and try to kiss her into agreeing with him. But it would be his will against hers and he would not do that to her.

"Thanks for listening. No doubt we'll see each other through work. Take care, Kristin. And remember, more than anything, I hope you find your happiness."

He walked to the door and let himself out, closing her apartment door behind him carefully. With every step to the elevator he felt as if he was leaving the most important part of himself behind. He'd known loss—his parents, Annie, Ben—but none of that was anything on how he felt right now. The elevator opened and he forced his feet to keep moving forward and stepped inside. The doors slowly began to close.

"Wait!"

A voice, Kristin's voice, and her hand came

through the closing doors and they sprang open, revealing her standing there. Tears poured down her face and she shook with emotion.

"I won't let you leave me again."

His heart broke on her choice of words, on the misery, the vulnerability and open emotion she revealed to him. She put out a hand and he took it, stepping out into the corridor with her and pulling her into his arms, where he knew to the very depths of his being that she belonged.

"I'm not going anywhere, not unless or until you want me to," he murmured against the top of her heads.

She still shook and he stroked her back, her shoulders, her arms. Trying to ease her reaction. It had taken courage to let down her defenses, to come to him, to stop him from leaving. When she settled, she looked up at him.

"I love you, Jack. I've never stopped loving you. Can we honestly work this out?"

"If we want it enough, we will. If we love each other enough, we will. I believe we do, don't you?"

She nodded, her eyes clearing as determination took the place of the unhappiness that he'd seen dwelling there since the first day he'd walked back into her life.

"I do, I love you. I want to make it work, Jackson. I want to be there for you. You don't ever need to be alone."

"I know that now. And I will be there for you, too. Always."

A door slammed, and Kristin looked around.

"What are we still doing here? Let's go into my apartment."

She led him to the apartment and locked the door behind them before leading him to her bedroom, where they slowly and carefully undressed each other. Each caress became a promise of a better, brighter future together, and when they joined as one, Jack knew that this was forever. This was them. This was the culmination of all he'd ever hoped for, all he'd never believed he deserved.

She loved him, he loved her, and that was enough.

* * * * *

Don't miss a single
Clashing Birthrights novel!

Seducing the Lost Heir
Scandalizing the CEO
What Happens at Christmas…

And the next installment,
coming February 2022
from Harlequin Desire.

COMING NEXT MONTH FROM

DESIRE

#2833 AN HEIR OF HIS OWN
Texas Cattleman's Club: Fathers and Sons
by Janice Maynard

When Cammie Wentworth finds an abandoned baby, the only man who can help is her ex, entrepreneur Drake Rhodes. Drake isn't looking to play family, but as the sparks burn hotter, will these two find their second chance?

#2834 WAYS TO WIN AN EX
Dynasties: The Carey Center • by Maureen Child

Serena Carey once wanted forever with hotelier Jack Colton, but he left her brokenhearted. Now he's back, and she, reluctantly, needs his help on an event that could make her future—she just has to resist the chemistry that still sizzles between them...

#2835 JUST FOR THE HOLIDAYS...
Sambrano Studios • by Adriana Herrera

The last man casting director Perla Sambrano wants to see is Gael Montez. But the handsome A-lister is perfect for her new show. When they're snowed in during a script reading, will he become the leading man in her heart just in time for Christmas?

#2836 THE STAKES OF FAKING IT
Brooklyn Nights • by Joanne Rock

The daughter of a conman, actress Tana Blackstone has put her family's past and the people they hurt, like Chase Serrano, behind her. But when Chase needs a fake fiancée, she can't refuse. Soon, this fake relationship reveals very real temptation...

#2837 STRICTLY CONFIDENTIAL
The Grants of DC • by Donna Hill

With her family's investments in jeopardy, Lexi Randall needs the help of real estate developer Montgomery Grant, who just happens to also be a notorious playboy. When the professional turns *very* personal, can she still save the family business—and her heart?

#2838 SECRETS, VEGAS STYLE
by Kira Sinclair

Cultivating his bad-boy reputation, nightclub CEO Dominic Mercado uses it to help those in need and keep away heartbreak. But when his best friend's sister, Meredith Forrester, who's always been off-limits, gets too close, their undeniable attraction may risk everything...

YOU CAN FIND MORE INFORMATION ON UPCOMING HARLEQUIN TITLES, FREE EXCERPTS AND MORE AT HARLEQUIN.COM.

HDCNM1021

*The last man casting director Perla Sambrano wants
to see is Gael Montez. But the handsome A-lister is
perfect for her new show. Now, snowed in during a
script reading, will he become the leading man in
her heart just in time for Christmas?*

Read on for a sneak peek at
Just for the Holidays…
by Adriana Herrera.

"Sure, why don't you tell me how to feel, Gael, that's always
been a special skill of yours." She knew that was not the
way they would arrive at civility, but she was tired of his
sulking.

She could see his jaw working and a flush of pink
working up his throat. She should leave this alone. This
could not lead anywhere good. She'd already felt what his
touch did to her. Already confirmed that the years and the
distance had done nothing to temper her feelings for him,
and here she was provoking him. Goading an answer out
of him that would wreck her no matter what it was. And he
would tell her because Gael had never been a coward. And
he'd already called her bluff once today.

He moved fast and soon she was pressed to a wall or a
door, she didn't really care, because all of her concentration
was going toward Gael's hands on her. His massive, rock-
hard body pressed to her, and she wished, really wished, she
had the strength to resist him. But all she did was hold on
tighter when he pressed his hot mouth to her ear.

"I've told myself a thousand times today that I'm not supposed to want you as much as I do." He sounded furious, and if she hadn't known him as well as she did, she would've missed the regret lacing his words. He gripped her to him, and desire shot up inside her like Fourth of July fireworks, from her toes and exploding inside her chest.

"Wouldn't it be something if we could make ourselves want the things that we can have," she said bitterly. He scoffed at that, and she didn't know if it was in agreement or denial of what she'd said. It was impossible to focus with his hands roaming over her like they were.

"I don't want to talk about it." *It. I* and *T*. She had no idea what the *it* even was. It could've been so many things. His father's abandonment, their love story that had been laid to waste. The years they had lost, everything they could never get back. Two letters to encompass so much loss and heartbreak. It was on the tip of her tongue to demand answers, to push him to stop hiding, to tell her the truth for once. But she could not make herself speak, the pain in his eyes stealing her ability to do so.

He ran a hand over his head, like he didn't know where to start. Like the moment was too much for him, and for a moment she thought he would actually walk away, leave her standing there. He kissed her instead.

Don't miss what happens next in...
Just for the Holidays...
by Adriana Herrera,
the next book in her new Sambrano Studios series!

Available November 2021 wherever
Harlequin Desire books and ebooks are sold.

Harlequin.com

HDEXP1021